My Little Shogun

My Little Shogun

This book is a work of fiction. Names, characters, places, and incidents are the product of the author's imagination. Any resemblance to actual organizations, events, or persons, living or dead, is entirely coincidental and beyond the author's intent.

Copyright 2022 by G.I. Gueco M.D.

All rights reserved. No part of this book may be reproduced, transmitted in any form, or by any means without written permission from the author.

If you purchased this book without a cover, you should be aware that this book is stolen property. Neither the author nor the publisher has received payment for this "stripped book."

ISBN 978-0-578-26450-9

Printed in the United States of America
Published: March 25, 2022

"To my dearest Abi, Nico, and Marco, never lose your sense of wonder."

Illustrator: Randy Ronald Clamaña

Editor: Abigail H. Crisostomo

    Lody D. Macatula

My Little Shogun

"He was a hero to many, and now all he wanted was to be a hero to Liam and me."

"Helping someone desperate while putting yourself in harm's way is the definition of a hero."

"There is much history in this place. It keeps me grounded and fills me with humility to be close to my ancestors."

"Knowing the past brings us closer to understanding the present and preparing for the future."

"People have forgotten how to champion goodness and how good it feels to help others. Pursuing what is good fills our empty hearts. You find happiness in helping others without expecting anything in return."

"I made it a point to forget the good things I have done to start fresh and do good things again the next day."

My Little Shogun

Author's Note

Sometimes, we feel alone even though eight billion people exist on earth. Every day we feel less connected to one another. We create an illusion that we don't need anyone. The truth is we allow ourselves to separate from each other.

Researchers might say that we are six degrees of separation or introductions away from any other person on the planet. Can you imagine that you are six or seven people away from meeting the President of the United States of America, the Pope, or the man or woman you were supposed to be best friends with or your happily ever after? Yet, no matter what you believe in, we sometimes choose to ignore how closely connected we all are.

Kudos to the men and women who achieved and discovered remarkable things in history on their own. Their absolute self-sacrifice to accomplish the impossible have helped us. However, isolation has its price. Though they have achieved more than others in their lifetime, great men and women in history are mostly unhappy. When we choose to be alone and not care for anyone else, a part of us withers away and dies. When we give into isolation and separate ourselves from other people, kindness and true happiness will be hard to find.

We must never ignore the chance that acquaintances could turn into friendships and relationships. It might be too late to realize how important they could have been in our lives if we did.

This book encourages us to value relationships without regard to their culture or appearance. It makes us remember how good it feels to take care of each other. No matter what life throws at us, we can rely on ourselves with the help of other people to pull us through. It reminds us to find happiness with the help of others.

    I want to thank my family, especially Abi, for helping me get through a difficult time in my life. Without them, I could have been lost and been in an abyss of emptiness. My dad died a year ago. The sadness that came after he was gone will be with me forever.

*   I know that you have always been proud of your daughter and sons. I know how you loved our mother so much. You loved her unconditionally. You were able to weather all the storms with the help of each other. We will never forget you, Dad. The lessons that you have taught us will be our inner voice. I miss our long conversations. I miss your smile. We miss you, Dad...Thank you for everything, and thank you for loving us unconditionally.*

*   We love you, Dad.*

*"To my beloved father, Jose Francisco V. Gueco,
you will forever be our hero.
We love you to the moon and back."*

Thank you!
May happiness and hope continue to find you

My Little Shogun

My Little Shogun
G.I. Gueco M.D.

My Little Shogun

Chapter 1
Celebration

GAMO HANZO

Fall was upon us. It was mid-October in Kyoto, Japan, where the leaves of the cherry blossoms showed their radiant beauty. Their foliage was a sea of colors that shrouded the hillside. The majestic blend of colors was reflected on the serene still waters around the Kinkaku-Ji, the Golden Pavilion. Fall's beauty was in its complete bloom as I saw the picturesque landscape surrounded by lush green trees. I felt the calm breeze that passed through the tree branches. And the sight of slow-moving water was enough to calm the most restless soul.

I held her hand as I guided her around the path towards the pavilion. "Gates," my pregnant wife was a sight to behold. She looked so elegant and regal. She held her belly as she descended the hill. Captain Katherine Gates Alberts, "Gates," was her call sign. Before we met, she commanded the Hercules 130, stationed in Yokota Air Force Base. She was nine months pregnant with our first son. Gates had complained lately of backaches that caused her to have a lot of sleepless nights. Gates wanted to visit the pavilion where we first met and, at the same time, get out of the house where she had been staying for the past few weeks.

Gates walked around the Kyoko-chi or Mirror Pond, where she could see the islands symbolically shaped like turtles and cranes. The careful placement of suitable rocks and pines created an illusion of a vast place. The place was serene. The sound of the slow-moving water created a sense of peace. Tourists started to come in, making the pace towards the pavilion slow. She glanced at me and gave me a huge smile. She looked so content and happy.

"I am glad that I am out of the house. Finally, I am getting some fresh air." Gates smiled as she rubbed her belly.

"He is surprisingly quiet and has not kicked my belly since I woke up this morning. He might be taking a nap." Gates continued the path near the rail which surrounded the paved road towards the Golden Pavilion.

Gates felt a sudden intense pressure on her abdomen that made her stop. She held onto the rail and paused as if waiting for something.

I saw her focus her eyes on the ground. Her once happy face now grimaced in pain.

"You are in a lot of pain. We need to go to the hospital now." I worriedly acknowledged how she felt.

Gates is in her third trimester, near her expected date of delivery.

She mustered enough strength to speak, "Hon, I think I am near. The contractions are getting frequent and stronger. Let's go to the hospital before my water breaks!" She painfully responded as she tried to breathe in between contractions.

I guided her back to the car as we left the Golden Pavilion that glowed in the background as the sun touched its walls. She walked carefully and felt her contractions increase steadily in intensity. Gates was tough. She knew what she needed to do; reach our car no matter how much pain she had. I pretended not to look worried. Instead, I fed off the strength emanating from my beautiful wife.

I held her hand tightly. I have prepared for this a million times in my head. The bag with new clothes for our son has been in the trunk of our car for a week. I knew the distance wherever we were at any point in the city. I thought of what route or streets to take to avoid traffic. I memorized the access line for the hospital's labor and delivery.

But no matter how much I prepared, there was still a sense of panic that I tried to tame as I helped my wife towards our car.

"Everything will be OK." My wife bravely reassured me. She felt that I was silent and saw my worried eyes. She knew me better than anyone. I might be anxious and scared, but I am somebody that you could depend on when the need arises.

We navigated the steps towards the direction where we parked our car. I let her sit in the back, so she has enough room.

"Hold on, Gates. I'll call Dr. Yami's office. I will let them know we are coming in."

She grimaced in pain and nodded. I tried to reassure her, and somehow, she forced a quick smile. Suddenly, I felt a warm, fuzzy sensation. Like a feeling that one gets when you know somebody cared for you unconditionally. Love was present in that moment. A gift that only a certain few could recognize and experience. And, in a few minutes, that love would be multiplied a hundredfold as we welcome our first-born son.

She was stronger than she looked. Gates' silky red hair compliments her blue eyes with delicate freckles on the bridge of her nose. Her smile could disarm you in a blink of an eye.

My Little Shogun

"Gates," as I fondly called her, is a Captain in the United States Air Force stationed here in Japan. Captain Katherine Gates Alberts has been here for five years now. We met at the very place we were visiting today. I met my other half, my one and only, that day.

Being a woman officer in the Air Force demanded utmost discipline and endurance. She always felt she should do better than most male counterparts. She took it upon herself to be the best in what she did, whether being a great example of what an officer should be or accomplishing her mission orders with precision and proficiency, which was close to perfection. She did not become a captain so quickly. She regularly was passed over for promotion by other colleagues. She never wavered. She persevered. She received the elusive Air Force medal of honor for her efforts in one of her missions. She would not divulge details of it, which was rightfully so.

I met her when she received a well-deserved weekend pass. She took it upon herself to enjoy Japan for its beauty and be a tourist for once. She decided to hop on the famous Tokaido Shinkansen-bullet train with top speeds of 199 miles per hour to go to Kyoto City.

Gates woke up early Friday morning to take the early scheduled departure of 5:57 AM. Gates had prepared for this trip and headed out of the base an hour prior with a Styrofoam cup with black coffee, just the way she liked it.

Today was instead an unforgettable day for her. She felt certain happiness as she exited the Air Force Base. It took a 40-minute hike to reach the Haijima station. There was already a group of people headed that way. You could hear excited conversations about places they would visit.

My Little Shogun

She hopped on the Tokaido Shinkansen. As she saw the countryside of Japan, she realized how beautiful Japan is. The ride was so comfortable that she did not notice how fast they were going. On the way to Kyoto, between Tokyo and Osaka, one could see the majestic Mount Fuji, which you could see when the train was near Shin-Fuji station. Wrapped around it were the farmlands east of central Fuji City. Though she woke up early and intended to sleep during the trip, she stayed awake and enjoyed every minute of it. As she sipped her freshly brewed coffee, she had a sense of calm mixed with the excitement of her upcoming adventure. She leaned her body comfortably on the back seat, smelling the aroma brought about by the tiny vapors emanating from her cup. She unconsciously let a deep sigh of contentment while she squinted as the rays of the sun touched her face. She was having a glimpse of true happiness without even knowing it.

Gates arrived in Kyoto a quarter before 10:00 AM. She did not know anyone in Japan. She grabbed her map and tried to find the route towards Miyako Hotel.

She stepped out of the train with her yellow Oakley backpack while holding a map with her right hand where she wrote the five places she would be visiting. There was no fear in this wide-eyed adventurer. Instead, she had feelings of wonder and excitement with the place she had called her second home for several years. It was about time she saw Japan's beauty for herself.

Gates registered at the hotel's front desk, and she knew beforehand that her room would not be ready for her. While she waited, she decided to start visiting Kyoto to enjoy its charm. Gates took a kogata (small) cab and directed the driver to take her to Fushimi Inari-Taisha. Gates turned a corner and was mesmerized by the sight she had seen, the adoration of thousands of famous vermilion torii gates. They lead into the dense wooden forest of the sacred Mount Inari. It has thousands of shrines dedicated to Inari Okami, God of rice. The gate structures were a sight to behold. One could see endless passages adorned with reddish-orange torii gates embedded in nature. The hike would usually take two to three hours, and you would often find yourself wandering around until you decided to turn back. You could quickly lose track of time.

Gates sat on a bench where one could see a bird's eye view of Kyoto, the Yotsutsuji intersection. Next, she took her map and found the famous Kyoto Ninenzaka Yasaka Chaya Starbucks, the first Starbucks in a traditional Japanese house with tatami seating near the Gion district. To get there, Gates took the Nara train lines, which connected other tourist sites in Kyoto. She arrived there around 2:00 PM, and before she was able to enter the establishment, she received a message from the hotel.

"Good afternoon. Your room is ready for you. Thank you!" Gates messaged them back and informed them she would get her keys later in the afternoon.

The Ninenzaka is a fusion of the old and new. So much history was in this 100-years-old-house. Gates enjoyed her pastries on the second floor, where there was an available traditional tatami seating. She wanted a quiet moment after several hours of wandering around Fushimi.

Gates then made the 10-minute walk towards the Gion district. You could see women fully dressed in colorful kimonos walking up and about the streets where traditional Japanese machiya (houses) were well preserved. They still had beautiful tatami mat flooring, sliding doors, and stunning wooden engawa (veranda). After several hours of admiring the district, she eventually ended her day and returned to her hotel.

My Little Shogun

On her second day, she forgot to set her alarm and woke up late, which was unusual for Gates. She was usually awake before 6:00 AM. It was a far cry from what she did daily. She lived a relatively structured life in the Air Force with endless routines and preparations meant to organize each day with a sense of purpose. It had been a while for her to enjoy a carefree day with no predetermined expectations. She surprisingly did not worry. She grabbed her map, where she wrote what she had planned to do. She planned to visit the Kenkun Shrine at Mt. Funaoka, where Oda Nobunaga was honored, but she slept most of the morning. She went back to her notes and saw a festival scheduled for that day. At noon, the Jidai Matsuri festival will begin near the Imperial Palace. The five-hour parade featured 2,000 performers dressed as samurai, ordinary people, and military figures from the earliest eras to the Meiji period.

Gates grabbed a quick bite in the lobby and headed out to the parade grounds near the Imperial Palace. The crowd was already dense, but she could still find an excellent place to get a glimpse of the parade.

A crowd gathered near the sidelines without anyone pushing to better their view. It is as if everyone knew where to go and created a space for others to have an opportunity to see the parade. Gates heard the "Oohs" and "Aahs" as performers threw their 20-foot spears up in the air to be caught by other performers. Colorful kimonos adorned beautiful ladies, which gave a sense of being regal. Army of shoguns or samurai marched ahead in unison, surrounded by sounds of drums and musical instruments before their daimyo.

One of them caught the eyes of Gates. He was wearing a Nanban-Gusoku, a samurai armor with a red cape. On his side were two swords (Daisho). The first one is a Katana, a long blade that was made to be decorative and at the same time deadly to their enemies. The second sword is the Wakizashi, a 12-inch dagger used for seppuku (ritual suicide). Nobunaga rode a majestic horse with prominent muscles. Oda Nobunaga's appearance gave you the impression that he was a significant figure in Japan. The history of Japan was unfolding right in front of the crowd's eyes. It gave everyone a sense of respect and gratitude to have an opportunity to see how rich Japan's culture and history were. Gates watched for a good 30 minutes more before she decided to go to the last place on her list.

She rode a bus and finally reached Kinkaku-Ji, the Golden Pavilion. I saw her holding a map close to her face trying to figure out where to go. I usually do not talk to tourists. But something in me pushed me to reach out and talk to her.

"Can I help you with anything? By the way, I am Gamo Hanzo." I shyly asked her while I was holding the side of my face like a nervous tic.

Gates was surprised and relieved that someone could fully help and communicate with her.

"I think I can help you." I tried to reassure her, considering I was a stranger.

"Thank you…" She let her guard down a little, and she unexpectedly let me help her. She gave me a timid smile, and I saw a couple of strands of her hair that fell in front of her right eye. She held the map with her left hand and casually tucked her long hair behind her right ear with her other hand. She looked so beautiful. As if time slowed down, I felt my heart beat a little faster.

Gates caught me staring at her and smiled as she repeated her question. "Do you know where I should go to visit the Golden Pavilion?"

My Little Shogun

I blushed and felt embarrassed. I tried to snap out of it and gathered myself back to answer Gates' question. "Yes! Yes! I can help you."

"Take this path around the Kyoko-chi Pond or Mirror Pond, where the islands look like turtles and cranes. It will take you there. It would be hard to miss. I know I am a stranger to you, but if you want, I could take you there." I continued.

Gates was about to hesitate and say no when suddenly a young boy hugged my right leg. He mistakenly thought I was his dad. I gently knelt and talked to the boy.

"Hello!"

While trying to hold my leg, the toddler accidentally let go of his blue balloon. I instinctively grabbed it and gave it back to him. The boy smiled and said, "thank you" in Japanese. Then, the boy's mother came rushing in, constantly bowing her head, apologizing to me.

"I am so sorry for my son interrupting your conversation. I am so sorry!" The boy's mother felt embarrassed as she apologized to us.

"He did nothing wrong. He is a sweet boy." I responded in English as I was being mindful of Gates so that she could understand. His mom carried him away while I waved back at him as they disappeared from a corner.

Her initial hesitation of letting me help her went away. She then smiled warmly at me. I gained her trust after seeing the kindness I showed to the boy.

I asked her again, "Sorry, may I help guide you to see it?"

Gates' eyes were now glowing with acceptance. She responded and said, "Yes."

Her eyes were fixed at me intently as I told her about the significance of the Golden Pavilion. According to his wishes, it was converted into a Zen temple by the son of shogun Yoshimitsu.

Gates asked. "How come you know so much about the Golden Pavilion?"

Before I could answer her, a group of older men recognized me and bowed their heads in unison. I bowed back to show my respect and to thank them. Gates was wondering why strangers would suddenly stop and recognize me. I kept the reason to myself. I just told her that they were distant relatives.

I started to open up to her. "I am a professor at a university, and I teach history. I will confess that I am a descendant of the son-in-law of the great Oda Nobunaga, Gamo Ujisato."

"I am impressed." Gates blushed in delight as she fixed her gaze on my embarrassed face.

"Yes, that is why I decided to study and teach my history - to understand my ancestors. Knowing the past brings us closer to understanding the present and preparing for the future."

We sat on a bench near the temple. "Let me tell you about the story of my great grandfather. Gamo Ujisato married Fuyuhime, daughter of Oda Nobunaga. He affectionately called him his little son-in-law." I chuckled as I said this. Another group of Japanese men approached us and bowed their heads in our direction. I stood up and said, "Arigato."

Gates noticed that strangers knew me. "It seems that everybody knows you."

"No, a lot of my neighbors are visiting these places during these times." I was trying to change the topic. She grew suspicious that people recognized me in Kyoto for something special, but she did not insist on asking me further.

So, I continued with my story about the significance of this place. "Oda Nobunaga was a daimyo (warlord) who was brutal to his enemies. He was well known for the battle of Okehazama, wherein he defeated an army of 25 thousand samurais with only two to three thousand men. He and his army outfoxed, outlasted, and outfought the most fearsome warlords of his time. However, he made a lot of enemies, including within his ranks. One of his men later betrayed him. During this time, he entrusted the care of his family to my great, great, great grandfather, Gamo Ujisato.

"Despite being a tyrant, he valued family and honor. During the few hours when he was about to be defeated and succumb to his enemies' attacks, Gamo Ujisato saved Oda Nobunaga's immediate family. They escaped before they saw the vengeful wrath of his enemies. There is much history in this place. It keeps me grounded and fills me with humility to be close to my ancestors."

"Seldom do people talk like that nowadays. You speak from the heart. I can feel the sincerity in your voice when you say that you are honored to be near your ancestors." Gates responded admiringly.

I blushed, and I tried to change the topic. "Have you visited Japan before? Or is this the first time you are visiting?"

Gates hesitated in answering but unknowingly trusted Hanzo. "I came from Yokota Air Base, and I am a pilot. I came here with a three-day pass. I decided to visit Japan and see its beauty for myself. So far, I am blown away by its charm and history."

"So… Have you been in Japan for a while?" I asked curiously.

"Yes. I just bought a map of Kyoto and decided to see five places." Gates replied.

"I am glad you took the trip, and I have the chance to meet you."

Gates felt a sudden warm pressure on her chest and felt butterflies in her stomach as Hanzo said those words.

We did not realize it was getting late, and I offered to take her back to her hotel.

"I think I will delay going back now. I was about to cancel my hotel and leave early."

"Why?"

"I want to listen to more of your stories." Gates grinned sheepishly. I could tell that she was getting comfortable with me.

"Would you like me to take you around and see other shrines tomorrow before you leave?"

"Yes, I would love that." She said with a wide grin.

"I will pick you up here around 8:00 AM tomorrow." We pulled in front of her hotel.

"I will see you tomorrow. Thanks for taking me to my hotel."

"You are welcome. I'll see you again." Gates got out of the car and walked towards the hotel door. She turned around and gave me the most beautiful smile as she waved goodbye at me as she was going in. As I drove away from her hotel, I thought, I had just the best day of my life.

Gates and I were now about to head to Kyoto university hospital. There was an inner turmoil of worry and anxiety within me. I held at bay my fear of not taking care of my wife and son. I finally mustered enough courage to stay laser-focused on the task at hand - to get to the hospital as fast and as safe as I could. We passed along the side of Kamogawa park before we crossed the Kamo river delta using the Kamo Ohashi bridge. It was a 15 to 17-minute drive. I ignored the signs as carefully as possible to reach the hospital quickly.

Finally, we reached the labor and delivery bay area of Kyoto University Hospital. Gates managed to smile, "it will be OK, Hon." She said this while the attendants pushed the wheelchair to the delivery bay area.

Now the wait.

At 12:01 AM, October 20, Gates delivered a healthy 8 lbs. 2 oz baby boy. As they showed our baby boy to Gates, she reached out and kissed him on his cheeks. My wife was exhausted but beamed with happiness. The next thing that happened, I will never forget.

Gates spoke to the nurse and handed our baby boy to her. "Can you help me introduce him to his father?" The nurse turned towards me and gently gave my son to me. I felt overwhelmed as I held my precious son for the first time.

"Hi, there! I am your father." As soon as he heard my voice, he looked straight at me as if saying, "Your voice seems familiar." I continued to talk to him as I started to sway from side to side.

"That is beautiful. You are trying to rock him to sleep. What is his name?" The doctor asked, smiling.

"We will name him Gamo Liam."

Chapter 2
Family

GATES

I have always loved flying. My dad, a licensed pilot too, owned a company that dealt with chartered planes. I spent most of my early years flying to different places with my family. I was his co-pilot on most trips. I remembered most of what we talked about during our flights. I cherished one conversation when he told me that life was like flying.

"You should always expect the unexpected but live in the moment. Before you knew it, your life could fly by so fast. You might miss it." My 5-year-old mind probably did not understand those words at that time. But those words made more sense as I grew up and matured. Life may have its ups and downs, but somehow, I knew I would always land on solid ground if I believed that I could persevere and surpass anything that life decided to throw my way.

I had bits and pieces of memories of places and mountain peaks we passed by during our flying trips. I remembered how everything seemed to move so slowly and gave an illusion that all things sat still. It gave you a sense of how peaceful it was once you were at 10,000 feet. It made you realize that no matter how big or successful you become, looking down from the clouds, you were just a tiny part of God's grand scheme of things.

I remembered my dad's words as he talked to me while I sat on his lap, holding the middle part of the "yoke," the airplane's control wheel. He would often teach me the purpose of each gauge in the cockpit. As he explained it to me, I nodded my head as if I understood while I twirled my ponytail with my hand.

"Do you want to fly with me today, pumpkin?" My dad asked me as he opened the retractable metal door, where behind it was my dad's favorite Cessna plane. My dad's name is Christian G. Alberts. He has broad shoulders and a black and white engine plane with a propeller tattooed on his right upper arm. His teeth sparkled as he smiled at me. His aviator glasses fitted perfectly on his face. He had a few stubbles on his squared jaw, but he still looked neat with his white cotton shirt. I loved flying with my dad. He owned a local company that operated a diverse fleet of jets with worldwide connections. My dad could bring a client to any destination they so desired.

"Yes, Dad! But first, let me check the propellers. Propellers are good. How about the wheels? They are good, checked. Everything seems to be OK, Dad. We're ready to fly." I confidently reported to my dad as I saw him smile when I pretended to start the pre-flight checklist that he had taught me.

We climbed aboard the Cessna 310, and my dad started to prepare for our flight. First, he clicked a switch to talk to the tower.

"Dad, when we go home, can we play?" I interrupted my dad before he had the chance to talk to the air traffic controller.

"Of course. We can play pumpkin. Of course. But we must bring the plane to St. Louis, Missouri for repairs."

"OK, Dad," I responded to my dad as I fixed my headset and got situated on my co-pilot chair. "My seat belts are on, checked!"

"Yes, they are."

"181 Sulu, Skies are clear, temperatures are fair, and...." The Air traffic controller talked to the plane in front of us as we waited for our turn.

"Alright, pumpkin, we need to finish with our checklist here. Make sure everything is green, radio on, flaps are up, and clearance is about to be obtained."

"Dad, are we there yet?"

"Not yet." He chuckled. "I will talk to air traffic control now, OK. Ground twin N881 Golf Charlie for departure, northwest request for taxi."

"881 Golf Charlie, walk around to taxi and by alpha 1800."

"Thank you, and we'll do the run-up."

"Make sure your seatbelts are tight and good. We are headed to the runway after this plane in front of us takes off."

Dad followed a smaller plane to the runway and waited for our turn. I grabbed my pink sippy cup and drank my Strawberry-Kiwi Kool-Aid.

My Little Shogun

As our turn to depart came, my dad positioned the Cessna at the edge of the runway. In front of us were the parallel bars on the ground. He set the power to 1700, checked if everything was green, and released the breaks.

"Going full power now. Now at full power. Gauges are all in green. Everything feels good. Wheel gears are going up, and now we are traveling in the wind." My dad talked to himself as he sped on the runway.

"We are doing good, pumpkin. We are in the air. So, look out, pumpkin!"

"Good job, Daddy!"

"Thanks, pumpkin!"

My father goes by "Tristan," which Mom fondly called him instead of Christian. Do not be fooled by his midwestern charm. He has the strength of three men and the focus of a hawk in achieving what he puts his mind into. He has relentless determination. My dad is a great pilot.

"Dad, I can see houses and buildings from here. But they look smaller, much smaller. You cannot even see people's faces from up here."

"Yes, pumpkin. You will have a different way of looking at things when you are way up here."

"I wish people would see what we see so that they will realize everyone is pretty much the same when you are up here. Maybe there will be no bullies if they see this."

"Pumpkin, is someone bullying you in school?"

"No, Dad. But my friend Alecx is. I told them to stop being mean to her because I remembered what you told me before, treating others the way I wanted them to treat me. I told them to leave her alone, and they stopped. I told the teacher, too."

"Oh, pumpkin," My dad started to become teary-eyed, and you could see from his eyes that he was proud of what I did.

" I am proud of you, kiddo."

"Thanks, Dad."

"People are people. They are not supposed to have checkboxes next to them. How you treat people should not depend on their appearance or where they came from. It should depend on how they interact with you or, better yet, who they really are."

My family taught me to treat everyone the same no matter who they are and their culture or background. I learned a lot in school. But kindness, integrity, and determination are taught every day at home.

There were a lot more flights and conversations that followed. Each one becomes an inner voice when I face the same situations. I will never forget them. They stayed with me until college and aviation school. Ultimately, I joined the Air force and became a pilot like my dad.

My Little Shogun

On the other hand, Hanzo also had a close relationship with his otousan (dad), Gamo Hideshi, who is married to Gamo Hana.

His mom would often take him to the university during lunch breaks to see and be with his dad. Mr. Gamo Hideshi was a history professor in Kyoto, Japan.

I remembered a story that my husband told me when he was young and on his trips to the university. First, he would recall seeing his dad surrounded by mountains of books around his desk while he reviewed his lesson plan for that day. Then, on one of his visits, he noticed a familiar book that his dad read to him every night when he had a chance to tell a bedtime story. A story that made sense to him when he was confronted with a problem when he was eight years old.

There was one time when he came home from school that he did not want to eat and just stared down on the floor. His dad sensed that something had happened at school. He tried to be patient with him and asked him to join him on a wooden bench near their enclosed courtyard garden steps.

"You look sad, and it's unlike you not to eat your supper. Did something happen in school? You can tell me, and I promise I will not be mad. I just wanted to know if I can help make you feel better."

Young Hanzo shed a tear from his right eye. "There is a bigger kid in school, and he took my lunch away. He said if I did not give it, he would punch and kick me."

"So, what did you do?" His father asked curiously.

My Little Shogun

"I told him that this is my lunch, and I would not give it to him if he forcibly would take it...But I would give it to him only if I wanted to. He wanted it so badly and took it when I offered it to him." Hanzo was furious and wanted to fight back, but he figured he would let it slide and not create a fight if he could. So, he did not eat and felt sad the whole afternoon because someone had done him wrong.

"Do you remember the story I told you each night about the ruthless and cunning daimyo, Oda Nobunaga? He had an impossible task like what you had. He was up against an army of 25,000 men against his 3,000 men. It was the battle of Okehazama. Legend has it that he passed by a shrine to pray because he knew it was a hopeless endeavor. Yet, he urged on with the impossible task with his belief in conquering his fears and faith in himself. Using the element of surprise, cloak of darkness, and a torrential downpour of rain, Oda Nobunaga surprised Yashimoto's army. His triumph catapulted him as one of the crucial Daimyos in Japan. He had a lot of battles and eventually succumbed to an enemy within because of betrayal. He knew he had a lot of enemies. He entrusted his family to someone he trusted and had the courage he had.

"My son, you are a direct descendent of the man (Gamo Ujisato) to whom the powerful daimyo (Oda Nobunaga) entrusted his family, including Fuyuhime, who became the wife of Gamo Ujisato. Ujisato's bravery spared Oda Nobunaga's family from the brutality of their enemies.

"You, my son, did the impossible like Oda Nobunaga. You had courage like him. However, you did even better than him because you figured out a way to win without fighting. You were able to stand firm but able to handle the bully well. You held your

My Little Shogun

ground without getting into a fight. You could control your emotions even if you wanted to do the opposite. You used your head. You did not allow him to bully you into a fight. To me, that was a great achievement, and you won. I am proud of you, my son." His dad then hugged little Hanzo and stayed silent underneath the Cherry Blossom tree.

Hanzo followed in his dad's footsteps and became a university history professor. On weekends he visited the shrines and historical places in Kyoto. He felt a strong connection to these places. However, he did not realize that he would meet his other half. *The one who would complete him and give him a son. A son he held in his very hands as I lovingly watched them from where I laid after giving birth to Liam.*

It was 6:00 AM in Kyoto, Japan, 4:00 PM in St. Louis, Missouri. Hanzo had spoken with my sister Sam while I was asleep. My dad chartered one of our jets and headed our way with my mom and sister. Hanzo's parents stayed as long as they could last night and returned the next day when visitors were allowed.

"Tok, tok, tok." Otousan knocked at our suite door and heard no answer back. He gently opened the door and saw all of us asleep. He saw his son at my side holding Liam's feet. Okaasan prepared a traditional breakfast for us and brought Omamori charms for Liam.

She gently tied it on his crib. A gift that symbolizes protection and brings good luck. It was a little amulet made of wood encased in a unique brocade bag.

Hanzo's parents were about to leave when I suddenly woke up and called out for them.

My Little Shogun

"Otousan, good morning! I did not realize you had arrived. I was just catching up with sleep. You should meet your grandson, Liam!"

Hanzo stood up and gently held Liam up. He cuddled him for a while before he gave him to his grandparents.

"We named him Gamo Liam. Liam, meet your grandparents." Liam opened his eyes and stared at them. They sat in a corner and talked to him. They were smiling from ear to ear, and they looked so happy and content. I suddenly felt a warm pressure on my chest. I could feel the love that they had for Liam.

"He has your eyes and nose, Katherine. He is so precious. Did you have a hard time delivering him?"

"It was difficult, but I was able to do it, especially with Hanzo by my side." I squeezed my husband's hand to thank him for being with me during this whole ordeal.

"I prepared some breakfast for you guys if you would like to eat?"
"Thank you, Mom."

"Did you have a hard time coming here? Jidai Matsuri festival is today." I asked since the hospital was in the center of Kyoto near the university.

"We were able to beat the crowds by using the back roads in coming here," Okaasan replied.

"That's good to know. Oh, okaasan(mom), I just remembered. Hanzo and I talked. We wanted to let you know that when Liam is one month old, we want a priest to bless him at a Shinto shrine. We want to pray for his blessing, Hatsumiyamairi. And after four months, have a baptism, too."

"Yes, that's a great idea, and we will help you with that. It is a belief that a baby blessed in a shrine will receive the protection of a kami. Each Japanese family originated from great ancestors, and I pray that our great ancestors will protect Liam. Our ancestors will be his kami, who will guide and protect him no matter what. Liam grasped Okaasan's finger and stared at her quietly.

"Are your parents coming, Katherine?"

"I just spoke to them. My dad is flying with my mom and sister to meet us here. So, Hanzo will be meeting them at the airport."

"I could get them and take care of them so that Hanzo can stay with you." Otousan offered to fetch my parents instead.

"Don't worry about it, Otousan. I will get them from the airport. Besides, I told Sam I would pick them up. They'll be here around 9:00 PM tonight." Hanzo insisted that he would take care of it.

"OK, Watashi no hokori to yorokobi (my pride and joy), I'll let you take care of it then." Otousan said to his son with a wide grin while he fixed his glasses. "But let me prepare where they will be staying tonight. I am pretty sure that they will be tired during the trip. So, I'll reserve two of the four Kyo-Machiya lodges we have so that they will be comfortable."

"No, Otousan, let them get a hotel. I don't want them to bother you." I reluctantly asked for him not to do that.

"It is my honor to welcome the parents of our daughter-in-law and the love of our son. Let me do this for them at least."

Okaasan (mother) insisted as well. "Let him do it, Katherine. They will be more comfortable there, and we will make sure of it."

"Oh my, I love you guys. Dōmo arigatō! (Thank you very much!)

Okaasan then offered to stay with me that night while Otousan and Hanzo ensured that my parents and sister's arrival would be as stress-free as possible.

Hanzo's family members are the salt of the earth. They would go the extra mile to make people they know feel like their own family. Since I have been here, they have treated me like their own daughter. I have always felt welcomed and felt that I belonged. Because of this, I am forever grateful that they found me, and I found them. They are family and will always be, no matter what.

It was almost 5:30 PM when I saw Hanzo get up to prepare himself to head to Kansai International Airport. It was a good 90-minute drive depending on traffic. His parents had left after lunch to prepare the lodges for my parents.

"Are you OK, Gates? Do you want me to get you something before I leave?"

"Thanks, Hanzo. I am OK. I feel the butterflies in my stomach. I feel excited to see my sister and my parents. I have not seen them for a long time. I am so happy they will meet Liam. They'll be ecstatic when they hold him in their arms, especially my dad.

"You know Hanzo. Dad was so happy that I married you."

"I thought he did not like me," Hanzo replied with a smirk on his face.

I grinned at his comment. "I know dad does not say much, but he respects you, and he is so happy how you took care of me when he is miles away from me. He felt at peace and contented when I told him how you took care of me when I was pregnant."

Hanzo's face flushed with that revelation. "I did not know that he thought of me that way. Next time you talk to him, say 'thank you.'"

"Hi! How are you guys! I am here. Okaasan came in as I was talking to Hanzo. He went up to her and spoke to her for a moment without me hearing their conversation. Then, he kissed his mom goodbye, and he headed towards me.

"I will be going. Mom will take care of you. Just let her know what you need, OK?!" He kissed me on my right cheek for the longest time I could remember.

"I will see you later, beautiful" He turned his back before he could see my lips say goodbye.

My Little Shogun

He started his drive towards Kansai International Airport and was anxious to be there in time. He wanted to be there before they landed. He did not notice that he was going beyond the speed limit. There was an unusual fog that night, and at times he could not see the car in front of him. Hanzo didn't notice a massive truck with a broken taillight was in front of him as he sped into the night.

At 40 feet, he saw a silhouette of the back of a truck, and he could hear his tires screeching on the pavement as he slammed on his brakes. There was no place to swerve and avoid the truck without hitting something. His eyes were now wide as lemons as he hoped not to hit the truck. Finally, his car was able to stop inches before colliding with the truck. The truck driver continued his journey, unaware that he could have been in an accident. Luckily for Hanzo, there was no one behind him. He started to move and said a little prayer to thank his ancestors for protecting him. He was now more alert as he neared the airport. At some point, he had to change lanes to avoid teenagers who drove out from parties after the festival in Kyoto. As he changed lanes, he would often turn on his emergency lights for a few seconds as a polite gesture of thanking the drivers behind him.

There were a lot of drunk drivers that night without regard to safety. Most were coming out of Kyoto from the festival. So, Hanzo decided to take the back roads and stay away from the highways to avoid them.

He reached his destination after more than an hour of driving. He parked his car in the airport garage while he waited for my parents to arrive. It was past 7:00 PM. He was still shaking from the near accident that he just avoided. He realized how life is so precious and unpredictable.

My Little Shogun

"Life will pass you by if you do not slow down to appreciate the things around you. Sometimes, when we have a lot in life that we should be thankful for, we tend not to appreciate how lucky we are. We ignore the many gifts that come our way, especially when facing difficult situations in our lives.

"All we need to do is to step back and see for ourselves what we have in our lives. Being grateful for your blessings will give you a different perspective about your life. So, today, I will continue to live my life with gratitude and learn to appreciate how lucky I am.

"Thank you, God, for my family. Thank you for giving me, Gates, and Liam. I am forever grateful to you, my heavenly Father." Hanzo pondered this thought while he waited for my family's plane to land.

Chapter 3
Little Shogun

GATES

It was a quarter before 8:00 PM in Kansai International Airport. My dad, Tristan, was preparing to land. He communicated with the airport tower as he began his approach. The skies were clear, and it was a full moon. The moonbeams acted like a spotlight that highlighted the airport. It had been almost 14 hours since they left St. Louis, Missouri.

"Kansai Tower, this is November 527 November Bravo. We are 15 miles east as we begin our approach."

"Yes, we see you, no traffic. Begin your approach to runway 24L, and we are ready for you. Great to have you back."

"Thank you."

Kansai International Airport (KIX) has spectacular views at night. You could see the lights on Osaka Bay which looked like a majestic painting on a canvas. As you begin your approach to land, you could see the tremendous effort to build this place on an artificial island. It always had the calming effect of seeing the beautiful nighttime sky with an endless number of stars blended into the linear silhouette of the sea on the horizon. In the middle of it all, you could see the arrangement of lights illuminating the landing strip that looked like a samurai sword handle. It was one of the most beautiful cockpit landing views you would ever see.

My mom, Elizabeth, was on the seat where I usually sat as a co-pilot. "The trip wasn't too bad. I can't wait to see Katherine and our grandson Liam!"

"Me, too. I can't wait to hold Liam in my arms." My dad replied to my mom.

"Sam, are you OK? We are about to land." My dad checked on my sister, Samantha.

"Yes, I am, Dad. Hanzo will be waiting for us at the gates, and I'll call him when we land. He and his parents already made arrangements for us on where we will stay."

"He did not have to. But knowing him now, he will go to extra lengths in making sure that we are comfortable. I like him, and I am glad that he is part of our family."

My dad had a flashback. He suddenly remembered when I called him about Hanzo for the first time.

"Dad, I met someone. I would love for you and mom to meet him." I called them out of the blue while Hanzo and I were still dating. We were starting to get serious then.

"It sounds like you really like this guy. You seldom ask us to meet guys you are dating." My dad laughed as he replied to me.

"Yes, but I need to tell you something. Hanzo is not an American. He is a local professor here in the university, and he's Japanese."

"Do you love him? Does he make you happy when you are with him?"

"Yes," I replied with no hesitation.

My Little Shogun

"Then that is all that matters."

I remembered our conversations about people coming from different cultures and backgrounds. My dad instilled in me that it doesn't matter where they come from; what matters is who they are and how they treat you.

I remember him saying, *"You first learn how to treat people around you at home. It reflects the way we raised you. Your belief in others demonstrates your faith in yourself. Your insecurities, how you deal with them, and how accountable you are for your actions affect how you treat people with different backgrounds and races.*

"Remember this, see people, not by the color of their skin but based on how they interact with you, how they treat others, and how they interact with their family. Resist the temptation to judge people you hardly even met and knew. To know who they are as persons is the best way to extinguish any bias you may have about their race."

My dad did not shy away from these conversations, and he knew that we do not live in a bubble where we are the only people on earth. He knew that I would meet different kinds of people, and whatever he taught me through his words would become my inner voice when I grew up.

"The word race was made by man and not by God. Whatever idea or structure that man makes changes over time. So, whatever your thoughts are about race can change. It is not absolute. Race is a label placed by human beings to sort people out. In the eyes of the Creator, we are the same because he created us in His likeness. To Him, the word race is nonexistent.

"How should we see people, Dad?" I interrupted my dad to know what he meant.

My Little Shogun

"Since we are all human, once we include race in our conversations, our biases can cloud our way of thinking. Therefore, we must know our tendencies to resist indulging them in how we see others.

"To be firm with your belief that all people are created equal is hard to do and not easy to achieve. Sometimes, we mean well, but we unconsciously use our biases in dealing with people."

My teenage self was listening intently to my dad. He rarely talked like this. I was nodding and was thinking of questions that I may have.

"Acknowledging is an excellent way to start. We should begin by acknowledging that we might judge people by how they look or based on what country they come from and who they choose to love. Knowing that we are capable of these thoughts might help us bite our tongue when we are about to say something mean or prevent us from doing something that we would regret later.

"When God taught you to love, he did not say love only one kind of person. He meant to love anyone, whoever they might be. You will make mistakes, but God is forgiving. He gives you a chance to recover and do a do-over, repeatedly without limits. I hope you pay attention. God might be speaking to you through me or others. You might miss him talking to you, especially in this fast-paced life we have.

"Life is like the Groundhog Day movie. Every day might feel like you are living the same thing every single time. But hopefully, you realize that he allows you to learn and recover from your mistakes every day or every minute, despite your many excuses. Loving others should be unconditional like how God *loves us unconditionally despite our shortcomings with other people."*

That was the last time my dad opened up to me about what he thought about race. But I could still hear how he said those words that night when we were seated out on the porch.

"Kansai tower, we are prepared for our approach." My dad talked to the air traffic controller (ATC) before landing.

"We see you. You are clear to land. Take the 24L runway."

"Gears down. Checking flaps. Harness secured..." My dad talked to himself as he saw the runway in front of him. He usually hums the Norah Jones song, Nightingale. He associated the calm of this song with the feeling that he experienced when he reached his destination safely.

"....Tell me your tale; Was your journey far too long hmm, hmm, hmm; Trying to tell me what to say; Can I fly right behind you? You can take me away.... hmm, hmm, hmm." My dad sang the song as he surprisingly knew the lyrics by heart. My dad was cool.

"400" Automated voice reminder of the distance of our CJ4 jet from the runway.

"100"

"10"

"Touchdown at KIX!" My family landed, and my mom sighed with a sense of relief after a long journey.

My dad had flown across the Pacific Ocean. With his flight plan just north of the Hawaiian Islands straight for 14 hours from St. Louis, Missouri.

My Little Shogun

"That was a good trip, and I don't feel tired at all." With a smile on his face, he kissed my mom on the cheek as he finished saying this with his deep voice. He was so excited and happy to finally meet his grandson and see me again. In front of them was the marshaller, assigned to our aircraft with a routine stop gesture with his red signal lights forming the letter X.

"You know, you were singing when we were landing?" Mom teased my dad about his singing of the Nightingale song by Norah Jones.

"Did I do it again?" He chuckled. His cheeks were red as an apple, and he had his happy eyes as he stared at mom.

"Yes. You did!" Sam squeezed my dad's nose as she interrupted my dad and mom's conversation. "Hanzo will be waiting for us at the gate."

"Alright, beautiful girls. Let's meet our handsome grandson, Liam." They disembarked their aircraft and headed to the immigration bay area.

"Good evening, Sir!" Welcome to Japan!" Ground personnel greeted my family at Kansai International Airport. They were bowing their heads (Ojigi) towards my family as one of the many traditions of Japanese people, emphasizing respect. It was like the gesture of respect in western civilization using a firm handshake coupled with a "Good morning" greeting. It was the same as holding the hand of an elderly family member and placing it on one's forehead (mano), emphasized by Filipinos as a sign of respect.

My dad, like a seasoned pro, bowed back to reciprocate their sign of respect to our family and flashed his oversized M & M (Midwestern Missourian) smile as they escorted them towards the airport. It took a while to finish immigration and gather their

My Little Shogun

luggage. Mom and my sister were ahead of my dad, pushing their bags with a push trolley.

"Welcome back, Alberts Family!" So written on a poster held by a man with two bouquets of yellow flowers in his left hand. He had chrysanthemum flowers loved by Japanese people. The flowers symbolized fall and were found everywhere in their October festivals. We would often associate cherry blossoms with Japan. But to the Japanese, chrysanthemum is seen in fall and is a unique symbol of the country itself.

Sam and my mom waved their hands as they saw Hanzo. They were so happy to see him and gave him the tightest hug ever. Of course, my husband blushed since he was not used to the affection, but it warmed his heart as he felt how loved he was by my family, although they were not related by blood.

He gave them the same respectful bow (Ojigi) they had received when they came in and asked my dad, "How was your flight? My family and I made sure you have everything you need with your stay here in Japan."

My dad stretched his hand as if to give him a handshake. Hanzo held my dad's hand with two hands tightly to show how much he appreciated his kindness to him. Then, my dad pulled Hanzo towards him and hugged him as if he were his young son, who he missed so much.

A beautiful sight to see like in any other airport, where happy meetings of friends and family took place. Every time I remember this specific moment of Hanzo's story when my dad met him in the airport, it gave me goosebumps. I wished everyone would treat each other like that. It reminded me of the feeling that I get every time I watch the YouTube video of the T-Mobile welcome back video at the Heathrow International Airport. I couldn't help getting teary-eyed when they sang Peters & Lee's Welcome home song near the end of the video.

"Welcome home, welcome

Come on in and close the door.

You've been gone too long

Welcome, you're home once more...."

Whoever made this video, and all the people therein should know that they were memorable and beloved for a heartfelt glimpse of how people could show love and care for others. I wished people could act like that all the time and give each other pure, undiluted joy.

Although we live in an imperfect world, the moment of undiluted joy that Hanzo had received from my dad's accepting embrace was enough for me to know that good will always be there no matter what life throws at you. I love them both so dearly.

"Trip was good. I had great company during the trip." He grinned and stared at Sam and my mom. "We are excited to meet Liam and Kate."

"I'll take you to them." Hanzo replied.

"No, it is late. I want Katherine and Liam to rest. And the hospital visiting hours are done now. We will see them first thing in the morning." My mom interrupted.

"Yes, I agree. We will see them tomorrow. It is almost 8:45 PM here. Thank you for the flowers!" Sam agreed with mom.

"Yes, thank you!" Mom held them tight and smiled at Hanzo.

"Lead the way, my son." My dad called Hanzo, son, for the first time.

"Yes. Let's go ahead. We have a little bit of traveling to do before we reach Kyoto." They chatted as they headed for the parking garage while Hanzo took over their push trolley.

Kyoto, Japan, was northeast of Kansai International airport, passing through Osaka. It was a good 61 miles away from the airport.

We headed towards the northeast exit of the island towards the bridge surrounded by the sea on both sides. It connected the island airport to the mainland. Everyone was so eager to talk and felt so excited about our trip. Mom and Sam, seated at the back, suddenly were silent. They fell asleep. Ahead was an 80–90-minute drive with light traffic.

Dad and Hanzo, seated in the front seat, remained awake while Sam and Mom were snoring during the road trip to Kyoto.

"Sorry, Hanzo. They do not usually snore as loud as this when they are with me at home." My dad blushed and felt embarrassed that Mom and Sam could not help passing out because of the long trip. They were running low on adrenaline and felt comfortable in the back seat.

Hanzo laughed softly and said, "Dad and mom are the same. But believe it or not, I find it soothing. It reminded me of my childhood rides with my parents when they could not help sleeping after a long fun day."

"Srnnk." My sister gave a loud snore as they passed a tollgate. My dad snorted in disbelief. Both chuckled like little schoolyard boys. "I think they like you and are so comfortable doing this with you inside the car." My dad tried to explain.

"I love it. Let Sam and mom rest. They look so peaceful and comfortable." My husband reassured my dad that it was OK.

"Hey, Hanzo. I've never thanked you. Thank you very much!"

"Thank you for what, Mr. Tristan?"

"Thank you for taking care of my princess when I am not around. It means a great deal to me that she met someone like you who puts her first before anything else, even forgetting yourself sometimes. Thank you for your sacrifices and love for her."

"You do not have to thank me, Mr. Tristan. I do it without thinking. She is like the air to me. I cannot live without her in my life. I expect nothing in return. I love your daughter to the moon and back."

"Thank you for being there for Kate. She will always be my little girl. How you took care of her meant a lot to me."

Hanzo was caught off guard but maintained his composure. He felt that his eyes were welling up almost into tears. "Those are kind words. She is my world, and I know she is yours as well. I will make sure that I will continue to love her unconditionally." My dad did not realize that Hanzo was open and honest about his feelings.

Hanzo continued, "Now I know from whom she got her sweetness and thoughtfulness."

"From his mom." Dad quickly answered back.

"No, from you, Sir."

"Hanzo, don't call me sir or Mr. Tristan. Call me Dad."

"OK, I will call you Mr. Dad then."

"Hanzo!!"

My husband was quick to deliver the punchline, "got you!"

Both couldn't help but smile throughout the road trip. Hanzo and Dad rode into the night, enjoying each other's company under the pale moonlight.

My Little Shogun

Chapter 4
Blessing and Gifts

HANZO

*A*t last, we have arrived in Kyoto, Japan. I did not expect that my father-in-law would care for me that deeply. I must tell my dad, Hideshi, all about this trip and how much kindness I received. Gates has been a gift to my life, but I did not realize that God continued to shower me with blessings by giving me, such wonderful in-laws. We might not be family by blood, but now I consider them part of my immediate family. I would treat them like I would care for my dad and mom.

"Are we near, Hanzo?" Mr. Tristan was still wide awake and entertained me with stories of flights that Gates and he shared. Gates' mom was still sound asleep, but I started to see Sam move.

"We just entered the Nakagyo Ward, home to the famous Nijo castle. (a 17th - century wooden shogun stronghold castle surrounded by lush gardens)." I was introducing him to the historical and magical place of Kyoto.

"You have a different system here in Japan. Are wards, subdivisions of large cities here in Japan?" Mr. Tristan seems to understand how different our addressing system is from the U.S.

"Yes, you are right, Dad. Japan has prefectures, municipalities/cities, and wards. Like your states, cities, and counties."

My Little Shogun

"We can't wait to take you to the Kinkaku-Ji (Golden Pavilion), Fushimi Inari Taisha shrine, Arashiyama bamboo grove, and many other cultural places. Kate was excited for you guys to come and see us."

"Can't wait to see her. I bet she already has a lot of plans for us and a list of places to visit." Mr. Tristan knew how organized and thoughtful her daughter was.

"Yes. You already have an itinerary that Kate made me memorize and recite back. She made sure I did not forget."

"Yup. That's my Kate!"

Sam was now awake but did not say a word. She was just smiling and listening to our conversations. It was quite a change from her busy schedule as an immigration lawyer in St. Louis, Missouri. She could now relax for a change. She is one of the most sought-out immigration lawyers in her country. She has helped countless lives who wanted to have a better life in the United States. She wore blue framed transition glasses, which complemented her sapphire eyes. She neatly ponytailed her red hair with a black scrunchie. She looked like her mom, Elizabeth, while Gates' look combined her dad and mom's features.

Gates is a redhead with perfect red lips. She has a slim face with a slender neck. Her eyes show a distinct bluish glow when you look straight at her. She loves to wear black sleeveless shirts that hugged her curves with perfection. She looks beautiful from any vantage point. She is my one and only.

I gently hit my breaks as I approached the stoplight and then signaled to turn left. As I moved forward again, Sam broke her silence. "There it is, Dad. The Machiya Hotel Fukune."

"Ahhh. She is alive!" Mr. Tristan was startled by Sam's voice. Sam giggled at his dad's reaction.

"I'll park near the entrance, and we will walk from there. I'll help you guys get settled."

A man wearing an elegant dark blue sports jacket with golden cufflinks approached us and brought a makeshift push trolley. As he came closer, I realized he was my dad, Hideshi, who waited for us to arrive to help welcome the Alberts.

"Good evening, Otousan!"

"Good evening, my pride and joy. I am here to help." My dad was smiling as he greeted me and searched for their luggage. Sam came out of the SUV and talked to my dad, whom she had already met during the wedding.

"Otousan, can I give you a hug?"

"Sure, beautiful Sam. Welcome back!"

Mr. Tristan then extended his hand to offer him a handshake. My dad grasped his hands with both hands while bowing and said, "I am so happy to see you again, Tristan and Elizabeth. Kate is so excited to introduce you to Liam!"

Mrs. Alberts then hugged my dad and replied," We can't wait for tomorrow to come to see them."

"Yes, yes. We will take you to Kate and Liam tomorrow, but you guys need to rest tonight. We took care of everything. Allow me to guide you to your lodges. We prepared two lodges for you. One is for you, Sam, and the other is for your parents."

"Thank you, Otousan," Sam replied as she followed him towards the entrance of the narrow pathway near the lodges. The path had a rough cement texture surrounded by a rectangular-shaped smooth surface in the middle.

In front of the entrance, there was a small minimalist sign of Machiya Hotel with the word Fukune letters more prominent than the rest. The alley to the lodges was different from any hotel entrance we had seen. But this was Japan, and they made use of every space available as much as possible. The walls surrounding the path had wires and tubes, which, if not adequately organized, could have been an eyesore. As they reached the end, Gate's family was amazed at what they saw. Four Machiya lodges adorned by a beautiful wooden lattice covered by roof tiles. There were simple plants and small trees that you would not expect to be there.

"Here we are. Sam, you will be in lodge D, and Tristan and Elizabeth will be in lodge C. Here are the keys, and I will help you get settled inside." My dad handed them the keys and led them towards their cottages.

I helped Sam to her lodge and placed her luggage near the entrance door.

"I think you all are tired from the trip. We will leave you now and rest. Everything you need is here, and my dad made sure of it. The bedroom is upstairs. I'll come back early in the morning to pick you up and bring you to Liam and Gates."

"Gates?" Sam smiled as she heard a different name for Kate.

"Oh, sorry. Yes, I like calling your sister, Gates." I felt embarrassed as I forgot that they did not know I called her Gates.

"That's cute. I like it. Thank you, Hanzo, and to your family. This place is beyond awesome!"

"It's our pleasure, and we are happy we can do this for you. No worries. We will take care of you. Just call me if you have any concerns or needs."

"Thank you!"

"Bye, Sam," I closed the door silently.

I saw my dad exit out of lodge D. We had the same intention of letting them rest after a long trip.

"I told them that you'll be here tomorrow late in the morning to pick them up since visiting hours in the hospital starts at 2:00 PM."

"Thank you, Otousan. Have you waited that long for us to arrive?

"No, son, just a few minutes. Let's go home. Stay with us tonight, and your mama will prepare you breakfast before we go back to Kate."

"OK, Dad. Thank you. Let's go." I placed my arms around my dad's shoulder as we walked together in the dimly lighted alley. My dad had a warm sensation of pressure on his chest. He had moments like this when he had a sudden gush of feelings of happiness and contentment. It made him also remember similar walks we had when I was still young. He held the hand I placed on his shoulder to show his appreciation for my affection as a son.

"I love you, Otousan."

"I love you too, son." My dad replied as we turned left towards our parked car.

Mr. and Mrs. Alberts were still standing in the receiving area of their lodge and stared at the interior of the Machiya Lodge for a few seconds. This lodge was utterly different from the places they stayed before. They had stayed in so many beautiful hotels worldwide, but nothing came close to this place. It boasts of beauty and peace at the same time.

"I can see a garden from here, Elizabeth. Is that a wooden washtub outside?"

"Look at that beautiful wooden floor. This place feels like a home." Elizabeth answered back while she walked towards the living room. She forgot that she had luggage to unpack and started to check out the unfamiliar setting of the lodge. She ventured to the spacious living room into the tatami room, which had a clear view of the wooden deck and garden. Mr. Alberts went upstairs to check on the bedroom and saw the beautiful beams and high ceiling adorning the open space.

"Wow, I never expected this."

While Gate's parents explored their lodge, Sam wandered around and found the bedroom. She threw herself in the bed, and after five minutes, she was fast asleep and snoring. Sam did not care to unpack nor change her clothes. She was out for the night.

Sam opened her eyes but had to close them again to prevent the glare of the spotlight from her ceiling from hurting her eyes. She forgot to turn off the lights last night. Sam struggled to pull herself up and decided to just sit at the edge of the bed for a moment. She thought she was going to work and was late for a second. She quickly realized that she was not and noticed she slept without changing clothes.

"Ring, ring." A faint familiar sound. It was the doorbell. She quickly went downstairs and opened the door. Her dad was up and asked her to come to their lodge to get breakfast. The Gamos ordered a special traditional Kaiseki breakfast meal for them, and it will be coming in 40 minutes.

My Little Shogun

"OK, Dad, I slept with my clothes on again. Haha. I'll be ready in 30 minutes."

Sam and her parents are now together. They were waiting for their breakfast to be delivered.

"It's been a while since I slept like that. I slept like a baby. I think you did too, Sam. You slept without changing your clothes again like you always did when you came home tired from school or work."

"Dad, did you tell on me again?" Everyone burst out laughing.

"Ring, ring..."

"I think the food is here."

"Good morning! Breakfast is here!" The chef spread the multi-course meal on the wooden table. It was a special breakfast. A senior chef meticulously prepared it. It included a Gohan - rice dish, Sakizuke - appetizers, Takiawase - vegetable course, Mushimono - a steamed dish, Nimono - lightly simmered foods, Yakimono - a seasoned fish course, Suimono/Futamono-a soup course and don't forget Mizumono- dessert. The meal commemorates a special occasion such as the coming of the family of Gates. Dad did not spare any expense in serving the best that Japan could offer. My dad wanted to make them feel special as they flew thousands of miles to be with Kate, Liam, and meet our family here in Japan.

"This meal is fit for a King! I don't know where to start?" Mr. Tristan's eyes moved from side to side, not knowing what to choose.

"Take it easy, Dad. We will get through it." Sam made a soft chuckle.

My Little Shogun

"It's been a while since we had a sit-down breakfast like this together. We should do this more often with Kate and Liam next time and with the Gamos, too." Elizabeth said this while pinching the belly of Tristan, who was not paying attention to her. He was overwhelmed on what food to taste first.

"Ooouuuch!" Mr. Tristan said, grinning.

Sam, Dad, and Mom were all seated around a small wooden table for a while as they enjoyed their colossal feast. They were laughing together as a family and enjoyed each other's company. It had been a while since they were able to do that. Elizabeth smiled. It brought back memories of when Kate and Sam were young and were still living with them. They are now at the empty nest phase of their lives. Then, suddenly, they heard a knock on the door.

"I think Hanzo is here to pick us up." Mr. Tristan said with his mouth still full of rice. He hurriedly tried to finish his rice bowl and got up to look at who it was.

Mr. Tristan opened the door and I saw a family enjoying a good meal together. It seems that they have forgotten their busy lives and learned how to slow things down for a change.

"Good morning! Sorry to bother you. I didn't mean to interrupt you guys."

"No, you're fine, Hanzo. Come on in. Thank you so much for this wonderful breakfast." Mrs. Alberts hugged me as I sat beside her.

"I spoke with Kate this morning, and she is so excited to see you guys. Liam will be there too when we come and see her."

"That's great. Let's hurry up and get ready to see Kate and Liam."

My Little Shogun

"No rush. Visiting hours start at 2:00 PM anyway. I'll come back. I just wanted to make sure you did not need anything." I reassured them to take their time.

"Yes, Thank you, Hanzo. I am so excited to meet and hold my grandson." She said with a wide smile on her face.

I went out for a while to do some errands and returned for them. Then, we all headed out to the university hospital to see my Kate and Liam.

It was 1:45 PM in Kyoto, Japan. One day before the Jidai Matsuri festival. There was light traffic in the streets, but this could suddenly change tomorrow. The once peaceful streets will have unending lines of spectators. They will see a parade of more than 2,000 characters representing simple peasants, daimyos (feudal lords), samurai to shoguns (military leaders appointed by the emperor) in colorful heavy clothing while on horseback. The different shades of characters were the ones that gave color to the rich history of Japan and helped build the foundation of Kyoto to what it is today.

A crowd filled the hospital lobby, and most would carry gifts and balloons. You could hear the happy chatter as visitors were allowed in. Unfortunately, I could not see Mr. Tristan since the giant plastic covering the Radio Flyer welcome wagon gift basket obscured his face. Mom (Mrs. Elizabeth) filled it with baby necessities and a big brown teddy bear with an airplane toy and a rattle with an airplane figure on it.

"I wonder who inserted the airplane toy in this basket. It was not there when I bought it." Mrs. Elizabeth bought the basket and knew that it was not there before.

"I don't know." Mr. Alberts answered back, pretending to be clueless while keeping a smile on his face. Mrs. Elizabeth just shook her head and smirked.

They finally arrived and opened Gates' room. They saw her with Liam. Gates had Liam's head pressed on her chest, sleeping soundly. Liam was fussy and crying this morning. But, when Gates pressed his ear on her chest, Liam immediately calmed down and fell asleep. Maybe the familiar sound of her beating heart that he heard when he was inside the womb calmed him down. It reminded him that he was not alone, and his mom would always be there for him.

"Saaaaamm!" Gates excitedly screamed as she saw Sam enter the door. Liam awoke and got startled too.

"I am so sorry that I shouted, Liam. There, there now. You are OK. We are all here." Gates tried to soothe Liam back to sleep.

"Saaam!" Now with her softer voice. She kept a wide grin on her face as she saw Mr. Tristan and Elizabeth followed Sam. Mr. Tristan cried as he saw his daughter. He has not seen her for a long time and has been missing her.

"Don't cry, Dad. We are all here now. Don't cry." She motioned for his dad and mom to come closer.

"I am so happy to see you, Kate." Her mom said as they approached Kate and kissed her on the cheeks.

I hurriedly removed my outer jacket, washed my hands, and placed a clean cloth on my chest to get Liam and let them share a moment.

"Thank you so much for coming. I missed you guys so much." She said these words while she hugged all three of them.

My Little Shogun

"We miss you and will never miss this chance to meet my grandson." Mrs. Alberts also had tears in her eyes as she talked to Gates.

"Let me introduce you to Liam." Gates smiled and motioned to give Liam to his grandparents.

"Wait, let me wash my hands first. I do not want Liam to get something from us." Mr. Tristan said. Then, he gargled with a mouth wash that he got from the hotel.

"Dad, what are you doing?"

"I don't want Liam to smell my bad breath." He replied with a loud chuckle.

I gave Liam, comfortably wrapped with a newborn swaddle, back to Gates. He was wide awake now.

"Liam, meet Grandpa and Grandma." She gently gave Liam to them. They went to the couch near the window where the baby bassinet was.

"Hi, pumpkin. I am your ugly Grandpa, Tristan. And this is your beautiful Grandma, Elizabeth. We finally met. We love you to the moon and back!"

"Look at those blue eyes. They can wipe all your worries away." Mr. Tristan continued in awe while marveling at his beautiful grandson.

Liam stared at them as he heard their voices for the first time. Mr. Tristan wrapped his arms around Mrs. Elizabeth while holding Liam close to her chest. Behind them, through the window, you could see that it was a cloudy day. But somehow, you could see some sunbeams escaping from a gap in between the clouds. It was a picture-perfect moment for Liam and his grandparents while the sunlight shone brightly on their faces.

I kissed Gates goodbye and waved at Sam. I did not want to bother Mr. Tristan and Mrs. Elizabeth. I stepped out quietly so they could spend some quality time with my Gates and Liam alone. I was happy to see Kate reunited with her family.

"Where did Hanzo go?" Mr. Tristan noticed that I was not in the room.

"He just left. He just wanted to step outside for a moment."

"This is cute." My mom was holding an amulet attached to Liam's bassinet.

"It is called an Omamori - like a lucky charm or amulet. It's a gift for newborns symbolizing protection from illness or anything that can harm them. Hanzo's mom got it from one of the shrines here in Kyoto. Thanks for bringing a huge gift basket. The teddy bear looks like Dad." Gates said, teasing Mr. Tristan.

"Did you see the toy airplane?" Mrs. Elizabeth asked.

"I bet dad placed it there." Gates knew that his dad loved airplanes, and he wanted to share their passion for planes with Liam.

Gates then continued to explain about my mom's gift to Liam. "The Omamori are Japanese amulets dedicated to specific Shinto kami. They are revered sacred spirits who could be the ancient ancestors of their entire clans. They believed that their kami would continue to guide and protect the generations after them. Gamo Hanzo has a significant ancestry. He is a descendant of Gamo Ujisato, a brave shogun retainer who saved the family of Oda Nobunaga from his enemies. Oda was one of the most revered daimyos in Japan.

"Hanzo is a descendant of one of the families who will be celebrated tomorrow during the Jidai Matsuri festival. I did not know that. He failed to mention that to me during our long car ride." Mr. Tristan was surprised and proud to have known a relative of someone important in Japanese culture and history.

"He does not tell this to anyone. So please do not tell him I told you. He will be embarrassed."

"Ok, we won't."

"By the way, how long will you be staying here?" Gates asked while looking at Sam.

"I took off for a month," Sam answered while holding Liam in her arms.

"Our board and managers will manage our chartered jets and company. I can communicate with them through the phone here. We can stay here as much as you like and spend time with you, Liam, and Hanzo." Mr. Tristan reassured Gates.

"That is perfect. We would like you to be here when Liam is blessed in a Shinto shrine when he turns one month old. It is called Miyamairi - a less known Japanese tradition to express gratitude and pray for his health and happiness. After that, when he reaches four months old, he will be baptized as well."

"We will be there, Kate. We would not miss it for anything else in the world. We will even fly back for his baptism." Mr. Tristan replied.

"All expenses to be paid by Dad, of course." Sam laughed as she joked around with Mr. Tristan.

My Little Shogun

"I am glad we are all back together again. I could not remember the last time we were all like this. I love you guys!"

"We love you back, pumpkin." Mr. Tristan replied and hugged her daughter.

The Alberts spent the whole afternoon together laughing and tried to catch up with things going on with their respective lives. Liam had brought two families together from different sides of the world. There is no other place one would rather be than with family.

It was 7:00 PM, and I came back with my dad. "Are you all ready for tonight?" I asked.

"Yes, thank you." Sam and her parents kissed Liam and Gates goodnight.

"I'll take them home tonight, Hanzo." My dad offered to take care of the Alberts.

"Are you sure, Dad?

"Yes, my pride and joy! Spend time with your family. I think tomorrow Kate and Liam will be discharged from the hospital."

"That's great news." Mrs. Elizabeth said ecstatically.

They all headed out to the door, and Gates' dad blew her a kiss before leaving.

"Did you eat yet, Hon?" I asked, concerned that she hadn't eaten supper yet.

"Yes, we just got done before you came. By the way, it was so nice of you to give me time with my family." She gave me a long kiss to say thank you.

"Can you do that again?" I said, teasing her. Gates smirked and pinched my love handles.

"I brought something for Liam. I got a clear glass locket to encase this." I said while showing it to her.

"What is it?" She asked curiously.

"Remember my ancestor Gamo Ujisato. This metal fragment was a part of his armor. It was passed from one generation to another, believing that he will be forever with us no matter what happens. It was given to me by my father. I will give it to you now, my son." I tied it on his bassinet while Liam was sound asleep.

"May you be protected and guided always. We will always be here for you...." I said a little prayer while looking at my son and caressed his forehead.

"I love you, Liam!"

My Little Shogun

Chapter 5
Decisions

GATES

The skies of Kyoto, Japan, at 9:30 AM, October 22, created a blue backdrop for the rising sun. The Kyoto streets had light traffic that would not be true for long. The Jidai Matsuri festival was about to begin within a few hours. Most locals and tourists anticipated this day and prepared to pick a spot on the parade route to get a glimpse of the festival. Some people wore traditional dresses while others were backpacking tourists in ordinary clothing. All would be grateful to see the beauty and splendor of the parade without them realizing that they came from all walks of life. Though the crowd seemed to be all from different backgrounds and cultures, they would all be the same for a rare single moment, with a shared common belief that this day was special.

The festival with more than 2,000 participants passed through Oike and Sanjo streets with historically accurate costumes in most periods in Japanese history, including the great Oda Nobunaga and his commanders. The 2-hour, 3-mile walk started from the majestic Imperial palace and ended at Heian Jingu Shrine. It attracted thousands of tourists and spectators who lined up these streets. However, the crowds were dense, primarily where the parade started and ended.

"Do you think they would send us home today?" I asked Hanzo over the phone as I finished my breakfast.

"I think so…Is Liam, OK?" Hanzo replied, and his voice was a little muffled. It's the voice you had when you had your phone pinned between your shoulders and cheek.

"You can call me back if you are doing something?"

"No, It's OK. I am just making sure everything is good. If the doctor finally sends us home today, Mom and Dad will prepare a welcome party for us when we get home."

"Sweet! I cannot wait to go home and bring this little munchkin home. I could not still wrap my head around the idea that we are Mom and Dad now." I bit the side of my lip as I said this to Hanzo.

"Yes, me too. It's kind of scary and happy at the same time. Being new parents does not come with an instruction manual. We will make mistakes, but I think we will be fine. I know that we will do our best to raise Liam in the best way possible. Plus, I have a beautiful and kindhearted wife. We are lucky to have Liam in our lives, and I am forever grateful." I got teary-eyed when Hanzo said these words to me.

"You are right. Oh, our beautiful son. We will take care of you." The door to our room opened as I talked to Hanzo. It was the nurse with the discharge instructions and papers.

"Liam and I are being discharged today."

"Let me hang up the phone so that you can listen to the nurse. I am on my way."

My Little Shogun

"No rush. Drive carefully. It will be a while before you get here anyway because of the closed streets. I'll see you in a bit. Love you."

"Love you too, bye,"

Hanzo took the northern path from the Nakagyo ward behind the Imperial Palace to avoid the closed streets for the Jidai Matsuri festival route. He avoided the vast crowds that lined the sides of the roads. The parade had already started when he reached the hospital.

Hanzo is 5 feet 10 inches tall with a rugged bodybuilder's physique. His hair is jet black with a natural curl in front. His sculpted body complemented by his square "hero jaw" gave him a noble figure. He lived by solid moral values similar to a Midwestern Missourian farm boy. He believed in truth, justice, and honor, no matter how inconvenient they could make you feel sometimes.

Hanzo was beloved in Kyoto, but he did not boast about it. He had received the rare "Kyoto Prize" for his work in philosophy and art. His medal with a noble tree in the middle adorned with red and green circular jewels was hidden inside a box where my husband kept his small childhood toys, sentimental letters, and old newspaper clippings about him. There was one newspaper clipping that mentioned his name. It was an article about him when he saved a toddler a couple of years before we met. After that, people in Kyoto, Japan, hailed him a hero. He jumped more than 20 feet into the water from a bridge to rescue a toddler whose car seat fell out of a car during a collision. He was a hero to many, and now all he wanted was to be a hero to Liam and me.

My Little Shogun

"Hi, Hon! Are you ready to go home? I bought a swaddle for Liam." Hanzo appeared through the hospital door with a bouquet in his right hand.

"Hello. We are here, too." Before I could answer him, my family came to see Liam and me.

"Did you guys have a hard time getting here? There is a big parade that just got started near the hospital." I asked.

"My dad and I avoided the route. We know the roads like the back of my hands. Besides, I am pretty familiar with where they pass." Hanzo winked as he replied and gave me the flowers. He kissed me on my right cheek.

"Can I tell them, Hon?" I asked.

"Go ahead." He grinned. I could see his cheeks getting red as a tomato.

"Every year, Hanzo looks like a knight in shining armor as he parades through the streets during the festival. He acts as one of the shoguns or retainers of Oda Nobunaga - one of the famous feudal lords in Japanese history." I said proudly.

"I told them I'll miss it this year because I don't want to miss the birth of my first son."

"Wow, Hanzo! I can't believe I have a famous brother-in-law." Sam shrieked in delight, accompanied by laughter from her and my family. Liam was startled by the sudden noise and started crying.

"I am so sorry to wake you up, Liam. You have an aunt who is crazy."

"You are so cute! Can I hold him, Sis? Is it OK, Hanzo?"

"Of course," I replied and gave Liam to her. Sam rocked Liam from side to side.

A wheelchair came in, and all was ready for Liam and me to be wheeled down for discharge.

"Can I take a picture of us…All of us. This picture will be the Gamo-Alberts family picture." Hanzo pulled out his phone to take a photo of us.

"I can take the picture, Sir. Everybody says: 'This is us and smile.'" The nurse was kind enough to snap a picture-perfect moment.

"Thank you." My dad bowed back to show his gratitude.

My dad had his happy eyes as he played with Liam while Sam held him. My mom Elizabeth hugged Okaasan and Otousan to appreciate their hospitality. I saw Hanzo had a wide grin as he saw my mom, dad, and Sam laughing with his parents.

"Look at us." I wondered. *"This is the way we should be around people that we thought were different from us. We might be from opposite sides of the Pacific Ocean. We might have had a different set of friends when we grew up. We might have different experiences and beliefs. But one fact holds - we can find common ground and learn to appreciate each other. We shared a moment where we did not think of ourselves as different. Instead, we considered ourselves as the same in mind and spirit. It was a moment of belonging and connection against all odds.*

Liam had brought two different families together despite the chaos of misunderstanding and misinformation that could exist around us when we let race separate us. Liam is a shining light for all of us. Thank you, Liam!"

Hanzo pulled in front of the hospital lobby as Liam, and I came out of the hospital. Otousan drove the other car behind him, where my family was.

"I think I got the car seat right. I spent an hour figuring it out. Please forgive me. It's my first time, but I think it is secure." Hanzo smiled as he carried Liam and placed him rear facing the backseat.

"Click! I think that is perfect." He was beaming proudly. He felt he had accomplished something big after correctly placing the car seat.

"Oh, Hanzo. You are too funny." I got up from the wheelchair and sat beside my son.

Liam was wide awake and was not making any sound. He seemed to be overwhelmed with all that was happening around him. Liam had a blue swaddle on with a double blue heart symbol on his right chest. He had a small rectangular quilted blanket that my mom made for him. Tied on his car seat was the glass locket with the piece of the armor of Gamo Ujisato inside it. Once we moved, he dozed back to sleep as we drove off towards the Gamo residence.

Traffic was slow as expected due to the ongoing parade just a couple of blocks away. As we turned right at an intersection, Liam woke up and looked at me. It was the same time I could see the long spears held by foot soldiers as men on horseback followed them. Although it was too far to see the details, I could see a man who towered above the heads of people in the crowd. I knew that he was a man of great importance because he had specks of gold color in his armor and headgear. I later realized that he was portraying Oda Nobunaga, one of my husband's ancestors. His family was saved and protected from their enemies by the Gamo clan.

"It sure seems busier this year. A lot of tourists came in to see the parade. It feels weird to see it from the outside. I got so used to being in it as one of the characters that I forgot how magnificent it is." Hanzo noticed the parade as well.

"Are you OK? Is Liam awake?" Hanzo noticed me checking on Liam.

"Yes. We are. Liam just suddenly woke up." I replied as I held Liam's hand and fingers.

"Maybe, he recognizes your voice. You talked to him every day and read him a book at night when you were pregnant."

"Maybe he does. He looks so handsome. I am glad he got his looks from me."

"Hey now. Don't forget about me." I saw Hanzo smiling as he looked at me in the rearview mirror.

We were a mile from Gamo's residence. They have relatives and close friends eager to see and welcome Liam into the family.

We finally arrived, and I always loved seeing the house where my Hanzo grew up. It was a beautiful Machiya house adorned with lattice windows, creating an illusion of bending light. It had lovely rooms with raised timber floors and tatami mat coverings. Unexpectedly, it had an open courtyard garden in the middle surrounded by wooden floors and narrow hallways.

Everybody clapped as we entered the house. We pushed the blue balloons on the floor as we thanked the 20 or so people who waited for us. Otousan and Okaasan prepared a welcome party for us. They set a large table in the middle of the room for all of us to dine. They hired people to wait on us and serve us a special multi-course meal (Kaiseki-ryori) which all of us could enjoy as we celebrated Liam's birth.

"Hey, Sam. Do you think it is OK to offer a toast of thanks during this dinner?" My dad was whispering while he asked my sister a question.

"It's not a wedding, Dad. But I think it's OK if you want to show your appreciation."

My dad stood up and spoke. "Good afternoon, everyone. I just wanted to show my appreciation to the Gamo Family." He raised his glass of sparkling Nihonshu (Sake).

"I want to say thank you for your hospitality. Thank you so much for taking care of our sweet Kate, especially when we were far away." Dad got teary-eyed and choked up while saying this. He then continued.

"Thank you to the people who are here at this party organized by Gamo Hideshi and Hana. We are happy and blessed that you welcomed us to your family and celebrated with us the addition of a new member to our family, Liam. So, I offer this toast to both Gamo and Alberts families. Thank you." He said with sincerity.

My mom kissed him and held his hand tightly. Those were the exact thoughts she had. Then, Otousan and everyone stood up unexpectedly.

Dad's gesture moved Otousan, and he began speaking as well. "You are so welcome. And thank you so much for being here and being part of our family" He and the other Gamo

My Little Shogun

relatives showed their heartfelt gratitude to us by bowing (Ojigi) at the same time to which we reciprocated.

"You all are going to make me cry. You guys stop." Sam broke the ice, and everyone started laughing. Everyone had a great time at dinner. We were all sharing stories and asking questions about American or Japanese cultures.

After dinner, everyone settled near the garden courtyard to drink some freshly brewed Japanese tea. Hanzo checked on Liam, who was in an adjacent room. He was still sound asleep and not bothered by the party. Hanzo saw me sitting on the wooden floors near the garden.

"You look so beautiful!" Hanzo had a grin from ear to ear as he sat beside me.

"You're such a liar. I feel that the doctor tore my insides apart after giving birth. And I feel so wasted from not sleeping well. But I will take the compliment." I smiled back at him.

"I love what your dad said. He appears to be tough, but there is some sweetness and thoughtfulness in him." Hanzo started small talk while sipping his green tea.

"I feel bad for him. He does miss taking care of me. I feel that he knows he is getting old and is missing out on the things that are happening in my life since I live far away from them." I hesitantly shared my thoughts with him. I knew that he might think we should move to the U.S. to live closer to him.

"But I have lived here all my life. So, I am not sure how I will handle being in the U.S." He suddenly became serious and stopped drinking his tea.

"I was not saying that we would move there. I just felt bad for my dad."

My Little Shogun

"But you were thinking about it…." He had that face when we were about to argue. There were a few seconds of silence, and then he continued after he gathered his thoughts.

"You know that's what I love about you. You speak your mind, and you are honest with what you feel. And I understand that you miss your family. I, too, would feel the same. So, if you want to move to the U.S., I will be there with you. I will be the happiest wherever you are." He held my hand and kissed it so gently.

"I am so sorry that I got irritated," Hanzo said with a flat affect.

"Here you go with that expressionless apology again."

"I can't help it if my face sometimes does not reflect what I say. I am so sorry." He said again with a devoid expression on his face.

"I was just messing with you. I knew you were sincere, and I got used to it. But honestly, I don't want to move. It would be better for us and especially Liam, to stay here. We will be happy here. Besides, we will visit them a lot anyways." I caressed his cheek as our lips locked together.

"Wherever you are, Gates, I will follow you."

"I know…"

"I love you, Gates."

"I love you too."

All of us were enjoying some quality time near the garden. My parents and sister were having a blast talking to Okaasan and Otousan. You could hear Sam's boisterous laughter whenever

Otousan tries to crack a joke. If heaven existed, I would imagine it would be like this.

"Hanzo, I am happy here like this. I might have done something good in my early life."

"Why do you say that?" Hanzo asked.

"Because I found you. And you found me. I might have done something good to deserve you."

"I think you had too much to drink. But, come to think of it, I do think you did something good."

"Ouch!!!" I pinched his love handles for what he jokingly said.

"Several years from now, I'll probably call it quits and retire as a captain from the Air Force. I want to concentrate on you and Liam. I can't be having more dangerous assignments and risk all of this."

"Are you serious about that? I will support whatever decision you make. We are a team now. I will be on your corner no matter what." He said reassuringly.

"Yes. I will be happy to end it as a captain. I will be happier to be with Liam and you all the time. Besides, there will be a lot of opportunities to fly in the private sector anyway."

"It would be nice to have you most of the time with Liam and me. Did you tell your dad yet?" He asked curiously.

"No, not yet. Dad will understand. He is like you. He will support me in whatever makes me happy."

"What are you two love birds up to?" My dad suddenly appeared out of nowhere.

My Little Shogun

"Nothing. We were just enjoying this rare relaxing time we have here. By the way, dad, thank you for that speech. And I miss you too." I gave him a big bear hug. He had a warm feeling of contentment on his chest, which he had not felt for a long time.

"Party was great, and we love your family, Hanzo. They are so fun to be with."

"They were all eager to meet all of you. And my relatives were all arguing where they would take you first for your tour of Kyoto."

"Can't wait to see Kyoto." My dad had his happy eyes and was excited for the coming days. He wanted to enjoy his time with Liam and was grateful for our whole family being together once again.

For several weeks, my family toured Fushimi Inari Taisha (A place of more than a thousand famed gates), Kinkaku-Ji (a serene gold-colored temple), Arashiyama (Bamboo Forest); Kiyomizu-Dera (a historical temple with picturesque views) and frequent visits to the Gion district for shopping and sightseeing tours. Hanzo, in addition, would drop them off weekly to ride the Shinkansen-bullet train to visit other parts of Japan such as Tokyo and Mt. Fuji.

Before they headed back home to Missouri, USA, Liam would receive a Miyamairi blessing ceremony in a Shinto shrine on their last week of stay.

"What is a Miyamairi ceremony?" My father asked me as he prepared the clothes that he would wear for the solemn ceremony for tomorrow.

"It's a tradition here in Japan to give thanks and ask for happiness and protection in a Shinto shrine when your son or daughter is between 30-100 days after birth. So, the Gamo family will ask their ancestors to continue to serve as kami for Liam. The kami is like a guardian or protector of their family."

"Ah, so it is a special ceremony. It's a good thing I brought my coat and tie." My dad smiled as he hung his clothes on his dresser."

It was about half an hour past ten in the morning. We were all gathered inside a Shinto shrine. Liam was all dressed up in a kimono and held by Hanzo. A Shinto priest knelt on the tatami mat in front of an altar. He started to chant and mentioned Liam's name in the middle of his prayer. Then, he did a ritual with several sticks on hand with zigzag papers and bells on them. He was praying for Liam's happiness and protection during these chants.

"Diing, diing, diing." The priest rang the bells during his chants.

"On the third ring, it seemed that time slowed down, and I got pulled away from my prayers. I traveled a long, narrow path of light and found myself hearing the bells of the Shinto priest as he moved his hand from side to side. I could not utter a word or move. I could see familiar things, but they seemed to have changed simultaneously. I was alone with my prayers for a long time. Now, I am overwhelmed with all the sounds and visions.

I feel my soul is attached to someone I am related to - a force I do not understand. Yet, I am with him for a reason. I have to be patient to know my purpose."

Unknown to everyone and for reasons no one can explain, a great ancestor, Kenji, became Liam's kami.

My Little Shogun

Chapter 6
Unexpected day

GAMO HANZO

As night fell on the 19th of October, the lanterns in the old streets of Kyoto were starting to light up. The sky had a purple hue created by the low sunbeams of the setting sun. At the same time, across the Pacific Ocean, the sun had already risen, and its beams bounced off the majestic St. Louis Arch walls. The bell of the Basilica of St. Louis, King of France, was unexpectedly ringing as the clock struck eight in the morning. Kyoto, Japan, was fourteen hours ahead of St. Louis, Missouri. My mom, Elizabeth, and Gates were on a conference call talking about Liam's upcoming 7th birthday celebration.

"Are you all packed for your trip?" Gates asked her mom.

"Yes. I finished baking the cake that Liam would love. It's an Avenger-themed cake." Elizabeth sent pictures via her mobile phone of the cake she made.

"It looks great, mom. We miss you guys, and we cannot wait to see you again. It had been a year since we last saw each other in St. Louis." Gates replied while she bit the corner of her lip.

"Liam is doing well and is included in the top 3 of his 1st grade batch. He made me promise this morning to tell his Nana how great he is doing and how he misses you." My mom kept her promise as she told Nana Elizabeth what her grandson wanted her to hear.

"I am so proud of Liam, and he is so sweet. What I enjoy most is reading books to him. I brought all the books that we read. Every time he reads them, I hope he remembers me." Elizabeth was teary-eyed as her chest swelled up with pride.

"We will all be waiting for your return. Tell Tristan and Sam that Otousan misses them both. He bought the finest Sake in town just for him." My mom said, chuckling.

"I will. See you guys there tomorrow, and we will call before we take off." Mom (Elizabeth) said goodbye and went again through her checklist of things for their trip to Kyoto, Japan.

A hissing sound of boiling water woke me up early in the morning the next day. My eyes were still half open and trying to accommodate the beam of sunlight from an open window nearby. It was a Friday morning, and I usually wake up first before anyone else. But today is different. I could hear Gates busy preparing breakfast in the kitchen. We slept late last night, making sure everything was ready for the surprise birthday party for Liam. We did not tell him that his Nana Elizabeth, Grandpa Tristan, and Auntie Sam were coming.

It had been seven good years since they were here for Liam's Miyamairi, a shrine blessing. We have been back and forth from here to St. Louis almost every year. We made it a point that Liam spent as much time with both of his grandparents. Most summers, Liam was with Nana and his grandpa in Missouri. He adjusted well with the Shogakko, Japanese elementary school system. Liam advanced to 1st grade with great accolades from his peers and teachers. Unfortunately, like any other kid, he was also exposed to bullies. I remembered a conversation with Liam, who went home sad one time after handing me a letter, asking one of his parents to meet with the principal. Gates also got a call from his teacher, who wanted to reach out to us regarding an incident in school.

I did not read what was written in the letter right away. Instead, I focused on Liam, whose face was so sad that day.

"Are you OK, Liam?" I asked him as we sat on the steps in front of our garden. There was a minute of silence from him. He was always happy as he came home from school and told me stories of his games with his friends. He was a happy kid and enjoyed school. I would often see him writing in his journal underneath the cherry blossom tree while talking to someone. He had an imaginary friend, typical to have at his age.

"Did something happen in school? I will wait for you to tell Dad. You can tell Dad anything, and we will try to talk it through. It will make you feel better when you talk about it."

Liam gave a deep sigh, "I… was pushed in the playground by a bigger kid after he took my handheld Mario brothers marble game from me."

At that very moment, I was about to burst into flames. I wanted to find and scold whoever pushed my kid, but I tried my best to calm myself. But, first, I checked if he had a bruise or which part of his body hit the pavement when a bigger kid pushed him.

"Did you get hurt?" He pointed to his back.

"I hit the metal bar of the slide as I was going down."

While touching his back, "nothing is swollen, and I don't see a bruise yet. Everything looks OK so far, but I know that you feel angry and sad at the same time. You are probably asking yourself why this happened to you." I glanced at the paper he gave me.

"Incident Report:

Dear Mrs./Mr. Gamo,

Liam pushed a kid today in school. After checking on the boy, he seemed to be alright. However, after talking to Liam, he told us that boy pushed him after getting his handheld toy. Since the boy provoked his actions, we wanted to reach out to you and talk about it tomorrow. Rest assured; we will speak to the boy's parents who started this all. Thank you."

"I know you feel bad right now. But, unfortunately, things like this are part of living. Bullying is always wrong. And what that kid did to you is a form of bullying. I am not mad that you pushed back. I am even proud that you were brave enough to react to an unpleasant situation.

"When you face a difficult situation like that, try to remember this…stay as calm as you can. Think first before you react. If somebody is about to hurt you, you have the right to defend yourself and push that someone back so that you can run away. I am also proud that you told me. It takes a lot of courage to do that. You keep on telling mom or me if something is bothering you. We will always listen to you and will not judge you."

"Yes, Daddy." Liam looks at me and hugs me tight.

"Sometimes, other people would try to put a label on you, such as you are a bad strawberry (weak). Please do not believe them. You and your parents are the only ones who know who you are. Sometimes, even though you are the smartest in the class, they will still bully you because you do not conform or be like the rest. Do not let anyone make you feel bad. You alone should decide on how you feel about yourself. When someone is bullying you, please never try to bear it. It needs to stop at the moment when the bullying starts. So, you tell your teacher and us about it, OK?"

"Yes, Daddy."

"If no one calls out bullying, the bully will not think of the consequences of his actions. So, when you become strong and confident, you should stand up for others. We will support you all the way, and we will always have your back. Do you understand, Liam?"

"Yes, daddy. I love you."

"I love you too, Liam!"

I was standing at the doorway of my son's bedroom as I recalled those conversations. I said a little prayer of wisdom and protection for him before waking him up for breakfast.

Liam looked so peaceful. You could see his jet-black hair and long eyelashes, which he got from his mom. Liam has a subtle mole above his lips. He also has a "hero's jaw" like me and a pointed symmetrical nose like his mom. He suddenly opened his eyes, and you could see his mom's blue eyes.

"Good morning, Dad. What are you doing standing there?"

"Just looking at you. I wanted to wake you up, but you look so cozy in your bed. So, I decided to give you an extra five minutes. Come on, let's get some breakfast and head for school." I said to him, smiling.

My Little Shogun

"Craacck, craacck," I could hear the wooden stairs as we headed towards the kitchen downstairs. I saw my wife's back turn away from us as we reached the first floor.

"Good morning. I see you two boys are awake. Come! Sit down and have breakfast." Gates was talking to us without turning her back.

"I need to fix those wooden stairs. You probably heard us going down." I grinned.

"Don't you know that moms have eyes on the back of their heads?" She winked at Liam and then looked at me and smiled.

We all sat around the square table facing each other. It had been a while since we had breakfast together as a family.

"This is a pleasant surprise. We seldom do this. Having breakfast together is nice for a change." I said to her.

"I just wanted to be with my boys before you head out. I miss having breakfast with you." Gates blushed as she said those words as if she was embarrassed to show how much she loved us. Even though she did not utter the word love, we felt it. I truly appreciated her kind gesture, and it was a picture-perfect moment for us as a family.

It had been almost seven years since Gates, and I had met serendipitously near the Golden Pavilion. A lot of changes had happened. Gates had served 12 years in the U.S. Air Force. She was promoted to Major before she voluntarily left and got honorably discharged. I remembered the night before she handed in her letter of resignation.

"Do you remember that conversation we had near the garden after I gave birth to Liam about me calling it quits from the Air Force?" Gates suddenly blurted out this question as we laid down on the bed, hugging each other after we made love.

"Yes, I do. What's on your mind?" I was surprised by her question.

"I have my letter of resignation in my locker for several days now. I want to talk to you first before I hand it in."

"You know where I stand. And it did not change. I am with you all the way. I have your back no matter what. If you get assigned to the coldest regions of Alaska, I will pack my bags in a heartbeat. I am committed to you. Everything around us, whether good or bad, is just secondary. You are the most important person to me. You are the reason why I wake up happy in the morning. So, do whatever makes you happy because that would make me happy too. I am all in."

Gates did not say a word for a few seconds. She was just looking up at the ceiling. I then saw her shed a tear on her left eye as she hugged me. As she held me tight, she whispered, "I love you." Then our lips locked.

When I had the chance while staring directly into her eyes with the end of our noses touching each other, I replied: "Love you back."

That night was one of my favorite nights I spent with Gates. It always sends a chill down my spine every time I remember that moment. That memory always made me wish for nights like that to happen a million times over.

Gates entered the private sector and worked for a Kyoto jet charter service. She became one of their best sought-after pilots while maintaining a work-life balance with Liam and me. She could not be much happier. Sometimes you just know that some people were born to do one thing which fulfills them completely. For Gates, it was spending time with Liam and me while doing what she is passionate about- flying.

I sat across Gates while Liam and I enjoyed the big breakfast she made for us. We were not used to eating so much in the morning. We were trying to finish everything since she woke up early to do this for us. I usually prepared breakfast for us. She often would still be asleep after coming in late from work. I would usually kiss her goodbye while she was in bed as I headed out to the university after dropping Liam off at his school.

On the other hand, I became one of the highest-paid university professors. Students, who would become leaders of Japan, attended my lectures. I became well known in Kyoto, but I ensured that this fame did not get into my head. I knew that I was doing something worthwhile. I was still the same guy who Gates met in the Golden Pavilion. I made it a point to forget the good things I had done to start fresh and do good things again the next day.

I took into heart what a famous athlete, Giannis Antetokounmpo, once said, "When you focus on the past, that's your ego. When you focus on your future, that's your pride. When you focus on the present, that's humility."

"I did not take anything for granted. But I did live my life daily without any regrets, especially after I experienced the fear of dying and losing it all after avoiding an accident after Liam was born. That incident shook me to my core. After that, I knew life could be short. And I better start knowing what is important: to live my life daily as if it was my last."

After the near accident with a semi-truck, I started making videos for Liam the day after Liam was born. Just in case I would not be around for special moments in his life - videos for every birthday, for every heartbreak I can think of, about the birds and the bees, his graduation, marriage, and about having a son or daughter. So, I continued filming without realizing I was creating a time capsule for Liam and Gates.

I could not believe my Liam was about to turn seven years old as I looked across the table. He had grown into a beautiful boy with deep-seated blue eyes, highlighted by long eyelashes. He had shiny black hair and teeth as white as pearl. Thanks to his mom, of course. She was very particular and made sure Liam brushed his teeth after meals, especially before sleeping. Liam was always excited about bedtime. He knew without fail that Gates would read him stories until he fell asleep. Maybe this was the reason that his imagination knew no bounds. I would often see him writing on his blue journal underneath our cherry blossom tree in our garden after school.

He often waves his hand in the air with gestures as if he was talking to someone. He then nodded his head before he wrote in his journals.

"What do you think I should write about, Kenji?" Liam asked a question while he raised his hands as I observed him once from afar underneath the cherry blossom tree.

"You should write about a ruthless warlord conquering unbelievers and destroying everyone who opposes his rule." Kenji replied with force while balling his hand into a fist as he raised it in the air.

"No, thanks. That is too violent. I should write about dragons instead." Liam smiled as he bowed his head and wrote in his blue journal.

My Little Shogun

"Whatever, Liam. You write what you want, but I think the story about the mighty warlord is better. Whatever you want..." As the leaves of the tree were falling to the ground, Kenji, who wore a full gear traditional gusoku samurai armor with gold and red specks at that time, shook his head as he turned his back away from him. Liam was smiling as he ignored the tantrums of his imaginary friend. He continued to write in his journal.

My Liam had an imaginary friend. Gates and I felt that it was normal for him to have one. So, we decided to ignore it and thought he might be helping our son to be creative as he wrote beautiful stories. He described his friend as a Golden Ryu or a Golden Dragon whenever we asked him to explain his imaginary friend instead of portraying him as a Shogun or Samurai warrior.

I did not know: *"Liam and Kenji had an understanding. At the end of each day they talk, Liam will forget how he looked and the details of what they talked about, especially stories about his past life. Kenji told Liam by the end of the day, he will remember him as a Golden Ryu or Dragon."*

Sometimes, Gates and I felt guilty that we could not give Liam a brother or sister, no matter how much we tried. I know that being an only son would have its challenges, such as being alone most of the time. Nevertheless, we tried our best to fill that void and give as much love as possible to make him feel less lonely.

"Thank you, Mommy, for breakfast. Ai shiteru, Mom!"

"Ohh...I love you too, son." It is not that often that Liam would say this. She kissed Liam as he stood up and helped me clean up the table.

"Ai shiteru too, Gates" I smiled and kissed Gates too as we prepared to head out of the house.

"What is going on? I am not used to all this sweetness. Are you guys, OK? I love you both. Take care as you go to school and the university, alright." Gates waved goodbye as we turned a corner towards the main street.

The early minutes before Kyoto, Japan's nightfall was a sight to behold and which beauty you could never get tired of seeing. The return of the purple sunset came into full view as it reflected on the waters on the sides of the bridge going to the Kansai International Airport where Tristan, Elizabeth, and Sam were already waiting for me. They had already landed, and I was about to pick them up. As I entered the loading area for arrivals, I saw a tall, smiling man with a white cowboy hat waving at me. I pulled up in front of them. As I got out, Mr. Tristan gave me the tightest hug that I ever had in my entire life.

"I miss you, son. Thank you for picking us up!" Mr. Tristan did not realize that he was still hugging me as he talked to me.

"Good to see you too, Sir. How are you, Mom and Sam?" Mr. Tristan did not realize that he lifted me when he hugged me. He was so embarrassed as he placed me down on the pavement.

"We're good! It is so nice to see you again, Hanzo. I hope we are not a bother." Mrs. Elizabeth responded as she pulled one of her carry-ons to the side of the car.

"No, don't say that. You are a joy to be with, and we always love having all of you around. Besides, Sake is all ready to be warmed up for you, Dad." He grinned at my remark.

"Well... let's go and see Kate, Liam, and the rest of the family." Mr. Tristan was already seated in front and ready to return to Kyoto while I help Mom (Mrs. Elizabeth) and Sam to their seats.

My Little Shogun

It was a beautiful Sunday morning. We adorn our house with banners and decorations. My mom, Mrs. Elizabeth, and Sam slept late last night preparing for this day. In the center was the Avenger cake that Mrs. Elizabeth made. Everything was ready except for the blue balloons I needed to pick up from the store this morning before the brunch birthday celebration.

"Everything seems ready. I will head out and get the balloons in time for the party."

"Do you want me to come with you?" Gates wanted to come with me since everything was ready, and she wanted to be with me.

"No, spend time with your family. They just came in, and you guys have been busy preparing. I got this. I'll be back before you know it."

"OK. Be safe. I love you."

"I love you too."

I drove eastward of Kyoto as I tried to avoid the highways. A few people were on the roads, and most were probably enjoying a leisurely, lazy Sunday morning after a week of hard work. The sky was clear without any dark clouds ahead.

I momentarily looked up at the sky, and I was enjoying a perfect day to be outside. Then, out of nowhere, hidden by a construction site, a yellow road sweeper appeared, which I overlooked, turning towards my direction. I suddenly turned to my left to try and avoid colliding with it. From feeling relaxed and without a care in the world, I suddenly felt my heart pounding as my wheels made a screeching sound. As I passed through the intersection after I avoided the road sweeper, I saw a middle-aged woman in the middle of the road pushing a stroller in the pedestrian lane. I had to aggressively turn my car to the left again in a split second to avoid hitting them both.

I suddenly felt weightless. My eyes widened, and my grip on the steering wheel tightened.

I felt a sudden worry and calm at the same time.

"I love you, Liam…Please take care of my Gates for me…"

With an abrupt, sudden movement of my steering wheel to avoid them combined with my forward momentum, my car was momentarily suspended in the air before it finally rolled onto the pavement.

My eyes were now shut.

My Little Shogun

Chapter 7
Hanzo

GATES

Next to my name in Hanzo's phone was the number 10, ten missed calls from me. His cellphone was unexpectedly intact on the road next to his car, resting against a corner of the building. You could see the bottom part of his car as if it was a toy car tossed up in the air then rolled several times before the corner of the building stopped its momentum of rolling. I had been trying to call him. Liam's birthday party was about to start.

I stood near the doorway with the phone in my right ear. I tried calling Hanzo again, but it just went straight to his voicemail after several rings. Liam and everyone gathered around a center table where the Avenger-themed cake that my mom made was about to be lit up. Friends and family came. Liam's friends were all excited to see the cake and were happy to be there with him.

Okaasan, Otousan, Mom, and Dad were looking at me. They had worried looks on their faces as I tried calling Hanzo again. I suddenly felt lightheaded with a cold sweat rolling down the side of my face.

Something was wrong.

Hanzo would not miss Liam's birthday party for anything in the world. At that moment, I was sorting out my worry that something happened to him and not extinguishing the joy that my

My Little Shogun

Liam had in his smile. I finally made a gesture with my hand, which Sam understood.

"I think Kate wants us to light up the cake and start the party," Sam told my mom, dad, otousan, and okaasan. Everyone nodded, and I saw Sam use a disposable lighter to light up the seven candles as everyone in the room started singing. As they sang "Happy Birthday," I could see Liam smiling and waiting to get a chance to blow his cake. I was still at the doorway with the hope that Hanzo would show up.

"Happy Birthday to you

Happy Birthday to you

Happy Birthday, Happy Birthday

Happy Birthday to you."

"Make a wish, Liam, before you blow your cake." Liam closed his eyes and made a wish. Then, with a single blow, he extinguished all the lit candles. Hanzo was still nowhere in sight, and I was beyond worried at that moment.

Okaasan noticed that the television in the kitchen was still on. There was breaking news on the bottom of the screen, which caught her attention. The flash news report was regarding an accident an hour ago. The information showed a white car similar to what Hanzo had. While she tried to get the attention of Otousan, my phone rang suddenly.

"Hello. I am Officer Hatani. I saw your name on the front of the phone of Mr. Gamo Hanzo, and you had several missed calls. Unfortunately, he was involved in an accident this morning. Are you related to him?"

"I am his wife. Is he OK?" I said nervously.

My Little Shogun

"He was rushed to the hospital." As the officer said these words, I felt my knees weaken before falling to the floor.

As I opened my eyes, Liam was in front of me. "Are you alright, Mommy?"

"You fainted, Kate. Take it easy for a while. There are police officers here ready to escort us to the hospital." Sam saw me collapse on the floor, and she rushed to my side. She picked up the phone in my hand when she noticed I was talking to someone and told them the address to our home.

I sat on the floor and hugged Liam. I tried not to show the fear in my eyes, but I thought Liam knew something terrible happened. We rushed to the hospital, and the doctor was already waiting for us. He sat us all down in a private room for families.

"I am Dr. Higashi. I am sorry to inform you that Mr. Gamo Hanzo already passed away when he got to the hospital. Nothing we could have done would have changed the outcome. I am sorry for your loss. And I know that it's important for families to say their goodbyes, and we prepared…."

Everything went blank, and I could no longer hear what the doctor said. All I could hear was silence even though he was still talking. I suddenly had a burst of uncontrollable crying without making a sound as I held Liam tight. I did not have the sense of time and place for a moment. I did not know if I was sitting or standing. I felt that everything was happening in slow motion, like I was suspended in the air. Liam felt it too and started crying even though he did not fully understand what was happening. I felt Liam was sobbing at my side, and it suddenly snapped me back to reality.

"I am so sorry, Liam. Mommy is here. I am just sad; that's why I cried. I am here for you, Liam." I tried to make a brave and calm face as I wiped my tears. Everyone just started hugging me. All I wanted to do at that time was to cry some more. But I had to hold it back just for a moment for Liam. I needed to be strong for him.

"Can his family and I see him and say goodbye to him?"

"Yes, we already prepared him, and he is in a private area for the family to be with him. Let me help you get to him."

I held my mother-in-law's hand as everyone walked behind us towards his room.

"Liam, you stay with Nana for a while, OK. I will just see daddy for a moment and say goodbye." I did not have time to explain what was going on. And honestly, I did not know how to break the news to him. There is no perfect way of saying that your dad just passed away to a seven-year-old.

"OK, Mommy, I will stay with Nana."

I saw Liam hugging his Nana as they sat on the chairs in front of the glass sliding door of Hanzo's holding room. I retracted the curtains and saw Hanzo lying face up, covered with a white blanket up to his chest. His face was peaceful even with the facial injuries he sustained from the accident. Tears began to fall again as I kissed him one last time on his lips. I pressed my cheek against his and whispered, "I love you, Hanzo! I will see you lat…." Before I could say "later," Liam came rushing in and hugged me as he reached out to grab his dad's hand.

"I love you, Daddy!" As he said that, I lost it. I did not remember what happened next as I found myself on the floor, sobbing as I hugged Liam tight.

A reporter from a local newspaper was in the hospital as well. He heard from one of his undisclosed sources who was an

My Little Shogun

emergency responder that Gamo Hanzo, one of the recipients of the elusive Kyoto Prize, died in an accident that morning. News about his death spread like wildfire in the local streets and Hanzo was mentioned in every local television breaking news throughout that day.

That day, an article in a local newspaper tried to account for what happened in that fateful accident.

"...One of our own, the beloved Gamo Hanzo, passed away today. He was on his way home carrying the blue balloons for his son's birthday. He confronted a choice in his efforts to avoid an accident with a yellow road sweeper, as witnessed by bystanders near the scene. Gamo Hanzo was about to run over a mother and child crossing a pedestrian lane as he avoided the road sweeper. To prevent running over the mother and child, he made a split-second decision of turning his steering wheel to the left, thus making him lose control of his car in the process. He was pinned down from his crashed car after it rolled over several times on the pavement and finally rested on the side of a building. He was pronounced dead at the site of the accident. We extend our deepest condolences to Gamo Katherine and his son, Gamo Liam, and his parents, Gamo Hana and Hideshi.

Gamo Hanzo was featured once in one of our newspaper articles wherein he saved a toddler from drowning. Today we pay our respects to one of the most remarkable men we have ever known. Even in his last few moments here on this earth, he chose to think of others rather than himself. To us, Gamo Hanzo is a hero. And would forever be a hero to us. We will never forget you.

Gamo Hanzo is a beloved husband and father. A man who chose to be selfless until the end. A hero in the eyes of many. It is with great sadness that we say goodbye to you. Thank you!"

My Little Shogun

It had been 30 hours since I last saw Hanzo on the hospital bed. Without the help of Okaasan and Otousan, I would not have been able to arrange a serene and beautiful funeral ceremony for my Hanzo. They had set a 24-hour vigil to be with him. It's locally known as the Otsuya or wake ceremony in western cultures.

"We set up everything, and you do not have to worry about anything. We are here for you." Okaasan reassured me as I sat with Sam, Mom, and Dad on my right and Liam on my left.

"Thank you so much! You lost a son too, Okaasan. I will be here for you. I love you like I love my mom. I hope you are, OK?" I saw the sadness in her smile.

"I am sad too, Kate. But the thought of seeing my son the happiest when he was with you and Liam gives me comfort. He was a good son and a great man. I cannot ask for anything more. I could have prayed even harder for Hanzo not to be taken away so soon, but I feel God needed an angel in heaven so desperately that he took our Hanzo. I trusted in God before to give us a son like him. I trust Him now to help us understand and get us through our sorrow of losing Hanzo so abruptly." She held my hand with both of her hands as she kissed me on my cheek.

"I love you, okaasan (mother)."

"I love you too, musume (daughter)." We hugged, and both cried on each other's shoulders. She then looked towards Liam.

"How are you, my son?" Okaasan turned her attention to Liam.

"I am OK, Baba (Obaasan-grandmother). Kenji kept me company. He told me Dad is in heaven already and said he will stay by my side no matter what."

Okaasan knew that Liam was referring to his imaginary friend, Kenji. She winked at Liam and said, "Can you thank him for taking good care of you?" She hugged him tight and said, "I will always be here for you too, Liam. Love you."

Unknown to and not seen by anyone except for Liam, Kenji, who is Liam's kami, has been standing next to him, holding the boy's shoulder to comfort him in his time of need. Finally, Kenji stood beside Liam and reassured him, "I will be with you. Everything will be OK."

In Liam's eyes, Kenji was wearing a black haori (light coat worn over a kimono) with a dark gray hakama (pants-like kimono) and a black obi (sash-belt-like clothing worn with the kimono). In addition, he wore zori (wooden sandals) on his feet. Seeing his friend Kenji gave Liam comfort.

"I know that I am invisible to others, and they treat me as a normal part of growing up. I know they think of me as your imaginary friend. Sometimes I don't even know if I am real, or they are right in saying that I am just part of your imagination. But I can assure you that I know that the feeling of me wanting to comfort you is real. If I had the power to take away your sadness, I would do it. All I can do is to be with you and help you get out of this sorrow as best as I can."

"You don't have to explain, Kenji. I am glad you are with me. Thank you for comforting me."

People around Liam were all focused on Hanzo's parents and me, and no one noticed Liam was talking to Kenji during the service.

My Little Shogun

A Buddhist priest started to chant a sutra while incense burned around him. Everyone was silent as they paid their respect and listened to the priest as he finished the ceremony. Unknown to the family and guest, an unusual event is happening outside. A large crowd numbering in the hundreds started to gather, waiting for the family. Men wore black tie suits, and women with children wore black dresses and clothes. All patiently waited for the family to receive them to offer their heartfelt condolences. Most of the people that came were not known to the family. They came after hearing the news that Hanzo passed away.

During the memorial ceremony, guests started to offer their condolences to the family. Then, each had a goriezen (specific ceremonial envelope) where they placed their okoden (money offerings). Then, before they were seated, they set their goriezen in a tray designated by the receptionist. Usually, guests do not talk to the family during the remainder of the ceremony.

Gamo Akira, sister of Okaasan, was patiently waiting to have a moment to speak with me while I greeted the guests.

"Kate, there is a vast crowd outside, and I think they also want to offer their condolences." She whispered.

"Let us ask them to come in," I replied as I was about to greet the last guest.

"They don't have an invitation, and they probably are worried about disrupting the funeral ceremony for Hanzo if they come in. Besides, there are several hundred of them, and they would not fit inside." Gamo Akira wiped away tears as she did not know what she would do next. People unexpectedly came uninvited and broke tradition, which was unusual for Japanese people.

"What do you want me to do?" My mother-in-law's sister asked with a trace of sadness and anxiety in her eyes.

"Those people outside came here for a reason. They came here for Hanzo. So, I will come out there with Liam and receive them."

As I walked out into the dimly lit pavilion with Liam, a sea of hundred specially-man-made lanterns lit up. The lanterns seemed to be floating in the air, probably because of the black background formed by the guests' attire. Everyone was silent. We were in awe of the sight and could hardly make out the faces in the crowd. Finally, an older woman approached us while we walked down the steps to receive and talk to them.

"Kono tabi wa goshuushou sama de gozaimasu (Please accept my condolences on this sad occasion.)." She was in her mid-70s and was holding one of the lanterns. She has almond-shaped eyes, which complimented her gray hair neatly tied in a bun with a black scunci. She seemed to know my husband, but I had never met her.

"Arigatou gozaimasu(a formal way of saying thank you). Are you a friend of Hanzo?"

"You're probably asking yourself, who is this old lady?" She forced a smile while she maintained a serious demeanor. "I am Takahashi Aika. When we heard of Gamo Hanzo's passing in the news, we had to come to show our respect and gratitude. Most of us here, at some point, have been given random acts of kindness by Hanzo. Though it might be small to others, it made a big difference in our lives. We will be forever grateful for his gift of kindness.

"I am a watermelon vendor. Hanzo passes by my stall every day as he goes to his work. I set up my shop early and had

My Little Shogun

difficulty carrying watermelon boxes, probably because of my old age. I am not as strong as before. But Hanzo would see me and pause to help me carry them every day even though he did not have to. He would even buy one and give it to someone in the streets. I know that act is simple, but it meant a lot to me. He gave me time. And I felt seen. He was one of the few that stopped when thousands would just go about their business. And because of his kindness, I was compelled to come and show my gratitude and respect." Aika then bowed her head towards us.

"Thank you so much for coming," I said as I bowed, acknowledging her sign of respect.

A couple then approached me and offered their condolences. "We met your husband several years ago during a train ride. There were no seats available together, so we had to sit in different seats. Hanzo was seated next to me and stood up and offered my wife his seat. When we got off the station, we had a chance to talk. We realized that we all work in the university. Since then, we would often have tea and talk about life and family. He became our friend." The couple bowed their heads too.

"Thank you for sharing this. If I knew, I could have sent an invitation for you both."

"It is alright. We felt that we needed to be here for Hanzo. Thank you for having us."

"I am not a friend of Gamo Hanzo, but I recognized his face in the news." After that, a middle-aged woman started to talk to us, too.

"I met him in a 711 store once. I was ahead of him in a line near the cashier. I was so stressed that day and needed to buy food for my four young kids. I was about to pay for the food and milk when I realized that I did not have money. In my haste, I

My Little Shogun

forgot my wallet. I started crying and was constantly apologizing to the cashier. Finally, I asked if I could put them back since it was my fault for not bringing my wallet.

"I felt so embarrassed. I did not notice your husband gave his credit card to the cashier to pay for everything. He then reassured me that it happened to him too and a stranger paid for his groceries. He said he was just paying it forward. I said, 'thank you.' He then smiled and left. I was not even able to ask for his name.

"I wanted to pay him back, but I did not know his name until I saw him in the news. Thank you for letting me pay my respects even though I don't have an invitation. Thank you. It means a lot to me that I can be here for him."

"You are welcome!" I felt overwhelmed and overjoyed at the same time. My husband did not tell me of all the good deeds. I remembered hearing him once when he prayed. He was praying to forget all the good deeds he had done for the day to do more tomorrow.

"I, too, owe a great debt of gratitude to your husband. I work with him at the university. I was once homeless. He showed me kindness like a brother would give his coat and shoes to his little brother when they had none. He helped me get a job at the university. I became a hard worker and continued to do so. It is one way of showing him how grateful I am for taking a chance on me. I did not want to disappoint him. Thank you!"

Before I could say you are welcome, a teenager carrying a lantern knelt in front of Liam.

"Hi, I am Kiyoshi. I wanted you to have my lantern." You could see a lighted candle in the middle of the lantern, giving an orange glow.

He stood and began talking to me. "Mrs. Gamo, I offer my deepest condolences. I do not know if you remember me?"

"Your face seems familiar, but I am sorry if I do not recall your name."

"I was the young boy with the blue balloon at the Golden Pavilion that your husband showed kindness to when I was still a little boy. So, I asked my mom to bring me here to say my goodbye." I was speechless, and I hugged him, saying, 'thank you.'"

I did not notice Liam started to walk towards the edge of the Tanji River and pushed the lighted lantern to float on the river. Then, the guests started putting their lanterns on the water, one by one. They wanted to pay respect to Hanzo, who had lived a good life. He was a great man to many.

Women, men, and children filled the river with hundreds of lanterns, like the Obon festival. They wanted to honor and remember Hanzo in a special way.

Meanwhile, across the Pacific Ocean, a group of friends, organizers of the RISE festival, came together at the Mojave Desert, 25 miles south of Las Vegas, at 5:00 AM, 7:00 PM here in Kyoto, Japan. My dad was best friends with the organizers. He asked them yesterday if he could get some lanterns to fly in honor of Hanzo. They knew how significant it was to honor Hanzo, so they offered to gather a group of people to fly lanterns.

"Ping, ping, ping."

My dad's cellphone alerted him of an incoming message. He showed me a video message of 20 people gathered and were about to release the lanterns in the air. You might say this was a coincidence, but I firmly believe that when a great man dies, the universe conspires to honor him.

We stood there hugging each other as we watched the lanterns float in the Tanji River while at the same time the lanterns started to fly in the middle of the Mojave Desert, halfway across the globe.

My Little Shogun

Chapter 8
Liam

LIAM

I stood in silence with my mom's hand on my left shoulder. I imagined my dad's face as I watched the lanterns float in the river. I will miss him. I did not fully understand what happened, but I knew that he was not coming back. I knew that I would not have the chance again to have those long walks with him every morning as we went to school. I knew I would not feel him kissing me goodbye during the weekends that he had errands to do when I pretended, I was still fast asleep. I would miss our numerous conversations. His voice would be my inner voice now.

One by one, people who were wearing black bowed their heads towards us as they said goodbye to my family and me. I saw my mom bow back to them as she tried to acknowledge their heartfelt condolences. If she could hug everyone who at some point met my father and experienced his kindness, she would do it. I was looking at her. I knew that she wanted to burst into tears, but she held back as she tried to accommodate the people around her who wanted to mourn with us.

My father meant a lot to these people. They were there to honor his memory. She knew that my dad was a good man, but she did not realize that he drew another big circle to include everyone he had met.

My Little Shogun

I suddenly remembered a conversation that I had with him when he wanted to emphasize a lesson in caring for others.

"We...you, me, and everyone else started to think only of ourselves when we were young. It is the "me principle." When we were babies, we cried to bring attention to ourselves to meet our needs. When we were hungry, we cried so that our mothers would nurture us, and we cried when we felt alone so that our father or mother would pick us up or cuddle us.

"We never once thought how hard it would be to raise a kid for the first time. We never thought there would be food on your neighbor's table as their father had lost his job the previous day. We never thought that people would be nice to each other even if they did not look the same. We only thought of ourselves, which is fine at the beginning for our survival. This belief is true until someone like me, your father, teaches you how important other people are in our lives. God did not create us to be alone. He made us find happiness with our contentment and joy in others.

"In a movie, a wise character named Tic Tic once said, "A good man draws a circle around himself and cares for those within - his woman and his children. Other men draw a larger circle and bring within their brothers and sisters. But some men have a great destiny. So, they must draw around themselves a circle that includes many, many more."

"What do you mean, dad?" My young mind tried to understand what my dad was teaching me.

"We all need each other. And for you. my little pumpkin, you can start by being nice to your friends or people around you in school."

"Even if they are mean to me?"

"Yes. Follow the three-strike rule like in baseball. Whatever they say, try to ignore them three times before you confront them. It would give them a chance to think of their actions. But if they raise a finger on you, you have all the right to defend yourself. That's why I enrolled you in a self-defense class. But if you can avoid being mean to others, please do so. Do you understand, Liam?"

"Yes, Daddy!"

Dad was cremated and laid to rest in a family grave. We all got home late, and my mom saw me yawning. I was seated at the dining table, and I did not realize I dozed off to sleep while I laid my head on the table to rest. I was waiting for my mom to help Sam settle in as she wanted to be with us that night.

"Come on, Liam. Let's get you upstairs."

I was so tired. I opened my eyes for a brief second, but I dozed back again to sleep. My mom, who saw how tired I was, picked me up and carried me to my bed. I woke up momentarily while my head lay on her shoulder. My dad usually was the one who carried me before when I unexpectedly slept while watching T.V. in the living room. Even though I was heavy, I did not hear my mom complain. Instead, she wanted to do what my dad did for me before. She tried to make me feel cared for, although my dad was no longer physically present to help us.

She carefully laid me in my bed, tucked me in, and covered me with my Star Wars Jedi blanket. Then, she kissed me on my forehead and headed for the door.

"Mom..."

"Oh, so sorry I woke you up." She turned around and sat at the edge of my bed.

My Little Shogun

"Are you OK?" My mom did not expect this question from me and sat there in silence for a few seconds. She did not seem to know how to respond or if she would cry in front of me.

"Oh, Liam. You are your father's son. You remind me so much of your dad, who was strong and sensitive to others' feelings before thinking of his own. We will be OK, and we will take care of each other like we always did before. That is what your father wanted for us. I love you, Liam!"

"I love you, Mommy! I'll take care of you."

"I love you too."

I turned to my side and fell asleep as I hugged the body pillow given to me by my dad last year.

"Good night, Liam." My mom responded while fighting back the tears. She rubbed my head gently before she stood back up and let me sleep.

I was a light sleeper like my dad. I could easily sleep anywhere and could wake up quickly. I heard the creaking noise of someone going down the stairs. My mom checked on me before she headed downstairs to prepare breakfast. I had my eyes open, and I was just staring at the corner of my room faintly lit by a small socket night light.

In the corner of my room was my antique red lacquer treasure trunk. It was here where I set aside my toys whenever my mom or dad told me to do so. A red ribbon hung on the side of the trunk, which I overlooked before. It was tattered and peculiar. It had a yellowish-green neon tape on its end that glows in the dark. But believe it or not, this was my dad's favorite color.

This sight made me stand up quickly from my bed and head towards my treasure trunk. I sat there holding the tattered

My Little Shogun

ribbon with the yellowish-green taped neatly around its end. The ribbon seemed connected to something inside the chest.

I opened my trunk and saw my BB-8 android, Millennium Falcon, and my Jedi lightsaber on top of the stack of toys that I had. The ribbon disappeared amid the pile, and I could not see where it was attached. One by one, I removed each toy from the trunk. Once I cleared the chest and reached the bottom, I saw a rectangular white box with my name written on top of it. Inside it was a portable DVD player with nine CDs labeled "1-9." Beside it was a necklace with a circular locket. In the middle was a piece of metal.

I opened a white envelope and saw a letter with a necklace.

"My dear son,

If you are reading this, you have found my surprise for you. I wanted you to have these. You have nine CDs with videos in them for each birthday you have until you are 16 years old. They talked about lessons I wanted you to learn that you may use when you become an adult. So, try to go through them each time you grow a year older. Life on earth is not forever, but the bond of a father and a son will withstand the test of time. If, for any reason, I am not thereby your side when you read this letter or when you watch one of the videos, rest assured that I am always there with you. Remember, a part of me exists in you forever.

Luke Skywalker in the Star Wars: The Last Jedi movie best describes it, "No one's ever really gone."

Everything you will hear from the videos is from my point of view. You will make your own decisions as you try to understand what I am trying to teach you.

My Little Shogun

Obi-Wan Kenobi once said to the young Jedi Luke Skywalker, "Luke, you're going to find that the many truths we cling to depend greatly on our point of view."

I have no doubt you will choose and do things wisely. Always listen to your mom, and whatever happens, she is always right. Lol. Love your mom and take care of her, OK.

I love you, Liam, and Happy, Happy birthday, my son!

P.S. I gave you my glass locket with the tiny metal of armor that once belonged to Gamo Ujisato. This amulet has been from one generation to the next. Now, I will give it to you. Take care of it, my son. Love you!"

I was dangling the necklace in front of me and tried to inspect the metal fragment in it.

"I will take care of it, Dad," I whispered as I wore it around my neck. I set aside the letter and played the first video of my dad. I remembered the same conversation we had about taking care of others.

"A wise character named Tic Tic in a movie once said, "*A good man draws a circle around himself ...* " I was about to watch it when I heard my mom calling out my name.

"Liam, is that you? If you are awake, I have already prepared your clothes. They are all in the bathroom. Come down here and eat some breakfast."

"Yes, Mom. I am awake. I'll come down in a few minutes." I set aside my dad's videos back in my red trunk and prepared myself for school.

My Little Shogun

I grabbed my yellow bag with a reflector and my yellow cap, which I usually wear as I walk to school. Then, I headed down the stairs, which still creaked as I stepped on them.

"Good morning, Liam. Sit down and eat breakfast!" I was not even surprised that she knew I was coming down. One of these days, when I am old enough, I will fix those stairs.

"I will be walking with you to school today and for several days. Please forgive your mom. I am not yet used to children here walking to school alone. I will get comfortable with it soon." She turned around and saw me wearing the necklace Dad had given me.

Kenji was surprisingly silent. He was just sitting beside me. I knew that I was the only one who saw him, but I would never get used to that. He would usually tell me stories about himself as I sat eating breakfast. I would just listen to him without saying a word. I felt that he wanted me to have quality time with my mom. He was wearing a gray kimono with a black belt. He had two swords neatly tucked on his sides. He smiled at me and pointed to my mom while pointing his other hand to his ear. I nodded to him without my mom noticing it.

"It's OK, Mom. You can walk with me. You will see that many kids in our neighborhood walk together and ride the train going to school. You can come with me, Mom. I know you just want me to be safe."

"I know parents here in Japan encourage independence at an early age. One of the ways is to allow young kids to walk to school. They built their communities to make it safe and allow that to happen. Having a low crime rate, excellent transportation for commuting, and at the same time, parents of adults in the

My Little Shogun

streets taught them to help in taking care of other young ones when the need arises.

I can rest easy that your dad will always be with you. I can see that you are wearing his necklace now. He loved that necklace. He told me before that he will give it to you."

I was surprised she knew that dad gave it to me. I held it and showed the glass locket with the metal fragment.

"Dad was funny. He used quotes from our favorite movie, Star Wars. I saw his videos for me, and I think he had one for you too. It was in my red treasure chest upstairs."

"Really?! Can I open your trunk and get it later, Liam?" My mom blushed. She knew that dad was making videos for me, but she did not realize that Dad made one for her, too.

"You can open it and get it, Mom."

"Thanks, Liam. Are you all set?" I nodded.

We switched off all the lights and headed out to the train station.

"I love your yellowish-green bag with an elephant design on it. Did you know that was your dad's favorite?" I was momentarily in front of her as she saw my bag with the red and blue alarm devices hanging on the side.

"Yes, he told me before. But did you know that he hung a tattered red ribbon with a yellowish-green tape around it in my red trunk? He knew I would be curious and discover that his surprise was attached to it. That was how I found the necklace and Dad's videos."

"That was smart of him. I like how he did it. Were you surprised?"

"It made my day. I loved how he did it."

We stepped out of the train station, and we saw a familiar face on the side of the street. Aika was trying to open her watermelon store. I ran to her and helped her transfer a chair near her watermelons. Once she saw our faces, she gave us the biggest grin ever. Then, she knelt in front of me so she could speak at eye level with me.

"You were listening. You are truly your father's son. Thank you for helping me." Takahashi Aika, the old lady who came to the funeral to honor my dad.

"You are welcome! I will see you tomorrow." I smiled back and hugged her. My mom hugged her too before we headed to my school, just around the corner.

Unknown to my mom, Kenji was walking side by side with us. He was still silent. He gave me a thumbs-up as I helped Mrs. Takahashi with her store. I would sometimes glance at him and would often see him with a surprised face even if he had walked before with my dad and me a million times already. He probably was so surprised with all the changes he saw compared to when Kenji walked these very streets when he was alive.

My grandpa and grandma would often tell me it was OK to have him as my imaginary friend. I was scared at first when I saw him, but I knew he meant no harm. But sometimes, I feel that he is real and knows things a real adult would know. I think there is a reason why I see him. He would show himself only to me and not to others. I am so happy that my family accepts the idea that I am seeing him while it might be frowned upon in other families. I remember my dad telling me to keep it to ourselves and our family. I should not tell other people because they might not understand. Kenji was not disruptive at all. He knew when to talk or interact with me. He let my life flow uninterrupted. Sometimes I even feel that he is sort of a guardian angel who my dad would often describe in his bedtime stories.

We reached my school. Teachers were already outside, greeting students as they walked into our elementary school. I placed my bag and things inside my cubby hole. Before I changed my street shoes to my school shoes, I hugged mom.

"I'll see you later, Mom."

"I'll be back and get you later during dismissal. I love you, Liam." She hugged me back.

"I love you too, Mom."

I went into my classroom and knew my mom was still standing outside looking at me. She had a worried look on her face and hoped that I had at least an easy day in school that day.

It was still early for classes to begin, and most of my classmates were seated at one end of a common waiting room. I sat opposite them where no one else sat. They were all busy chatting with their friends and telling them about different family trips over the weekend.

As I sat alone, I took out a book from my bag. "The Alchemist," which I promised Dad before, to read ten pages every time I was not doing anything. While I tried to read it, I overheard my classmates' conversations.

"We went to Super Nintendo World at Universal Studios in Osaka last weekend with my dad."

"We were there, too."

My Little Shogun

"It was a lot of fun, especially with my dad playing all the different games they had there. It was like you were inside the games that we played. I am so happy that my dad took us there."

"How about you? Did you have fun there?" I heard their conversations while I read my book. I promised my dad to read each day. I bowed down, and I did not let them realize that I was listening to their happy conversations. I wanted to be sad, but the memory of my dad smiling while he read this book to me prevented me from feeling unhappy. Instead of frowning, I was smiling as I remembered how my dad read it with a different tone of voice to make it more interesting.

I knew I was alone on the opposite side of the room. I put my head down to not attract any attention to myself. I could hear the happy cheers from the other side simultaneously with the silence sitting beside me. I was getting used to being invisible until a voice out of nowhere prevented it from being permanent.

"Hi…. What are you reading?" I was startled and did not know how to respond. She was standing still in front of me while waiting for my response.

"Is it a good book?" She persisted, and she was patient with me. Her name was Emma. The prettiest girl in the class tried to talk to me. When I say prettiest, I do not know if she had physical attributes that made her beautiful. At a young age, my definition of being pretty is through how they act or how kind they are to others. I do not know yet what physical features you need to be pretty. In my mind, if you are kind to others, you would be appealing to me.

"Yes, it's a good book. My father gave it to me. Have you read it yet?"

"No. I was just curious about what it is all about."

"It is about the magical adventures of a shepherd named Santiago in pursuit of his personal legend. At least, that was what my father said. I have not read the entire book yet. But I promised my dad to read ten pages every day until I finish it and tell him after if I like…."

"I read that book already." An older boy suddenly interrupted our conversation. The older boy, Ryo, was the brother of Emma. He was a known bully in elementary school and was in grade 6. Stealing lunches and pencils from little kids is his hobby.

"You are the kid on T.V. Sorry for your loss. Mr. Gamo Hanzo was a good man." I did not expect that conversation to come from a bully. I did not realize at the time he had a heart. Maybe when he saw his sister talking to me, he showed pity on me.

"Can we sit with you?" Emma and Ryo sat beside me. And the once noisy room became silent. The prettiest and the one regarded as a bully in school sat with me. Another student stood and went to my opposite side then sat beside us. And then the rest followed. Once they were all on my side, they began to chat with their friends again. I was no longer alone in my corner. That simple act of befriending me, by the most famous student and the bully, was enough for the rest to take notice.

"I am Ryo, and her name is…."

"Emma. I know." Emma blushed as I knew her name.

"Maybe after I read it, I can let you have it as long as you give it back."

"That's so nice of you. I am curious to read it. Thank you." Emma gave me a beautiful smile that can erase one's all fears and worries.

"You are alright, Liam. We will find you during lunch and will sit beside you to eat. OK?"

"OK." And the teachers started calling their students in their classrooms to begin their class.

"See you later, Ryo. Emma let us go to our class. Mr. Hiro is calling for us."

"See you later, brother." Emma waved goodbye.

I went home that day eager to tell my mom what had happened to me. Although my dad had just passed away, my mom was somewhat happy that I had at least an OK day in school. Instead of being sad and being alone, my mom was relieved that at least something good happened to me.

"Mom, I met some new friends in school today."

"What are their names?" My mom was eager to know who they were.

"Emma and Ryo."

My Little Shogun

Chapter 9
Beginnings and Ends

GAMO HANA

It was late October, and everyone was enjoying the season's colors. Every shade of red, orange, and yellow mixed with fading green colors was scattered all around us. Everyone was excited when autumn came. I love this season, but I barely noticed it this year. I missed my son Hanzo.

Everyone was so busy. The world continued and did not stop when my Hanzo passed away. Indeed, the universe would not stop for anyone. Life would go on, no matter what happens. Soon, my Hanzo would be a memory, and others would even forget him. But to me, he is my sun and moon. Without him, I spent my days wandering without any sense of time. I wake up each day, counting each breath I take. I count the number of hours I forgot to shut my eyes to sleep and rest. Living felt useless. But I had to pick myself up and try to be strong like my Hanzo. He would not want to see me like this.

My Hideshi still needs me. He would not say much, but I could tell the joy in his eyes left him the way it left me. No parent should ever experience burying their child. It should be the child burying their parents and not the other way around. Life is not fair. Just when we thought we fully understood how to live life, it would find a way to humble us. It would constantly remind us that we know so little of what life is all about.

"Good morning, Hana. I see you did not sleep well again. How long have you been sitting here?" Hideshi saw me seated in front of our house as I watched people pass by.

"Not long, I could not sleep again…." I quickly answered even if I did not remember how long I was seated on this wooden chair.

"Here is some tea for you to keep you company." Hideshi carried a wooden tray with a cup filled with powdered green tea leaves (matcha) and a pot of hot water. He sat beside me and prepared my cup of tea with a bamboo whisk.

"I'll join you shortly." He said before going inside the house again. He probably forgot something.

The sky was blue with specks of white clouds. The once empty street is now starting to have a few people walking its paths. I saw Emiko across the street sipping green tea as well. I waved at her as she saw me doing the same thing. Her granddaughter and grandson lived with her. Their names were Ryo and Emma. They both go to the same school as Liam.

Children started filling the street slowly with their backpacks on. They were either in groups or sometimes alone. I saw a glimpse of a mother with her child at her side out of the crowd. Gates and Liam were now in front of our house. Liam and Hanzo used to walk this way as they headed to the university and Liam's school. They would often stop by and say hello to us.

Now it's Liam and Gates who would say "Hi." I miss Hanzo. A memory of him flashed in my head for a moment as I saw them approach me.

"Hi, Baba (from obaasan, which means grandmother)." Liam greeted me as he kissed my cheek.

My Little Shogun

"Good morning, my Liam. Do you want some tea, Kate (Gates)?"

"Thank you, Mom. We are walking our way to school. I want to go with him today. But I would let him do it on his own later." She replied, smiling.

"You can do it. Right, Liam?" I hugged Liam as I asked him this question.

"Like a walk in the park, Baba. Dad and I did this a million times already. And he taught me how to do it too. He would walk behind me and let me lead." Liam forced a smile.

"We will go ahead, Mom. Don't forget about dinner. We will see you later."

"We won't. You take care. We will be there." I smiled and waved at them as they made their way to school. Liam turned around and gave me a flying kiss before they disappeared out of sight.

My Liam is such a thoughtful boy. Gates and Hanzo raised him well. After 5 minutes, Emiko waved at me again. Then I saw Ryo and Emma come out of their house and head to school.

Unknown to everyone, Emiko and I talked about Liam. I was worried about how he would be in school. I was unsure if he would just keep to himself after what happened. However, I knew that Emma was in Liam's class, and Ryo looked after her when they were in school. So, Emiko promised to talk to them to look after Liam.

Emiko talked to both after telling them a bedtime story. Emiko knew that they might be too old for bedtime stories, but she believed in teaching them life values through storytelling.

My Little Shogun

"Sobo, what story do we have tonight?" Emma asked.

"Yes, what story, Baba?" Ryo was also curious.

"It's a part of a story or poem from a different land by Thomas Macaulay. It's about a Roman army officer, Publius Horatius Cocles. They were about to face defeat and began to cross the Tiber River.

In the face of impossible odds,

"Then out spake brave Horatius,

The Captain of the Gate:

'To every man upon this earth

Death cometh soon or late.

And how can a man die better

Than facing fearful odds,

For the ashes of his fathers,

And the temples of his gods...'"

"What lesson can you get from Horatius' words?"

"To be brave when the odds are against you." Ryo quickly responded.

"Yes…Be brave in defending your beliefs. To believe in what you think is good even if everyone around you is against it or thinks differently." I wanted them to learn this lesson, and I thought of adding what Hana asked me to do.

"I know that you are not a Roman soldier, and you would not experience what Horatius did. But his bravery in defending what he believed was good and true could be applied to other situations in life."

"How Grandma?" Emma asked.

"Hmm… Let me think of a situation that would apply to you. I got it. For example, a lonely boy is reading a book on one side of the classroom or cafeteria in school. Nobody seems to want to talk to this boy. What is the bravest thing that you could do that would be good for him?"

"Talk to him and befriend him so that he would not be lonely anymore," Emma responded.

"You got it. You got what the story wanted you to learn and how you could apply it in your everyday life. I am so proud of you both." Emiko was so happy but did not give any specific instructions to her grandkids to help Liam. Instead, she wanted them to do it naturally and do it because they believed that it was the right thing to do. In doing so, their actions would be sincere, and the lessons learned would be long-lasting.

As we gathered around for dinner time, I heard Liam discuss meeting Ryo and Emma. He was surprised that they wanted to be friends with him. Liam was almost content in reading his book. He did not realize how good it felt when someone wanted to be friends with him. Liam unexpectedly felt a sense of support, especially during sadness. I sat in front of him as he told his story about his friends. I did not say a word. Instead, I smiled and knew I made the right choice to talk to Emiko.

Sam, Elizabeth, and Tristan were all there too. They would stay for a couple of months while Elizabeth would stay six more to be with Kate (Gates) and Liam.

My Little Shogun

Routine became my friend. Every day I sit on my wooden chair as I waited for my grandson to pass by on his way to school. Liam has been going to school by himself now. He would always say hello and kiss me before he went to school. Then after a week, I noticed that Liam was no longer alone. Now, he came back from school with Ryo and Emma. Even if I am still grieving, the sight of those kids together gives me a glimmer of happiness. It's a joy to see Liam has found friendship.

As they went home from school, he saw me sitting in front of the house again. He stopped by, and I never forgot our conversation that day.

"How are you, pumpkin! How was school?"

"School is OK. I spend my break time with Ryo and Emma most of the time. They keep me company."

"Are they your friends now?"

"Yes. Sobo, can I tell you something?" He asked.

"Of course, pumpkin. What's on your mind?"

"I miss Dad…." He said sadly. I could see the longing in his eyes.

"I miss him too. We can talk about it. They say it is better to share what you feel, especially when someone you care about died." I did not want to discuss Hanzo's death indirectly, such as using phrases like passed away or lost a loved one. Instead, I wanted to be direct as much as possible to give Liam a chance to grieve.

"I miss walking with him when I go to school. It's a good thing Kenji keeps me company."

My Little Shogun

"You still see your friend? What have you guys been talking about?" I knew that Liam had an imaginary friend, and I did not mind it at all. I even think it was good for him. Honestly, it was another way of support for him.

"*Kenji said that kids are the forgotten mourners. He said that adults often forget two things: 1. If you don't see kids grieve, it does not mean they don't. And 2. Children suffer too like adults. But they grieve in their own way.*

"*I asked him how long I would grieve, he said 'for the rest of my life.' I thought grieving was terrible. But he told me to treat it as something good. Adults often would be afraid to talk about death, fearing that it would worsen.*

He said, 'it's the other way around. You should not feel shame nor be afraid. They will always be there watching over us even if we do not see them.'

"*It was similar to a story of a kid who had a mother who died. Before she died, she said to her son: 'Every time you see a butterfly, I am there visiting you. The butterfly is like a memory. It comes and goes.' As long as I have memories of my dad, I will never be alone. He will always be with me. He is me and is a part of me.*"

I was amazed at how deep their conversations were. It was like the great speeches of Kate Atwood and Carly Runestad about grieving. I have also been grieving, and I made a conscious effort to acknowledge that Liam grieved too.

"Kenji is right. We are here for you no matter what. Death ends a life but being the son of Gamo Hanzo would never change. It is always OK and great to remember and miss him. You can always come to me, and we will talk about it as long as you like."

My Little Shogun

"I would like that, Sobo. I love you."

I hugged him and kissed his right cheek. "I love you too, Liam." Right there and then, I knew Liam would be OK. We spent the whole afternoon talking about the good times we had with Hanzo. Then, I called Kate to tell her that Liam was staying here for a while and both of us would join them later.

Seasons changed, and people moved on, but the feeling remained. It would have been close to five years since Hanzo died. Liam was in grade six and was still friends with Emma and Ryo. Time flew by, Liam grew up and became a sensitive and loving young man. He still has his shiny jet-black hair with his blue eyes highlighted by his long eyelashes. Liam still would place his hand behind his neck every time he felt embarrassed, just like his dad did when he was young. Liam's appearance is somewhat different from his classmates', probably because of his blue eyes.

All these years, when I saw Liam, I had one fear and would not want Liam to experience - bullying. Being different and not conforming to how others look, or act would sometimes result in bullying.

Saying that bullying does not exist in any school is a lie. Bullying in schools exists in any country. Japan was no different from other countries where bullying could exist without being appropriately addressed. I was a teacher once, and I had seen bullying upfront.

I prayed every day for Liam. If somebody tries to bully Liam, I will likely intervene. I thought our afternoon talks helped me take care of Liam and gave me a sense of whether he has done well in school or not. I felt other kids would not understand him. Kids who have one of their parents die would be different. Unlike students who still have their dads with them, Liam would not have a father figure that he could identify with or rely on for support. He could not experience the love shown by a father specific for each age or circumstance after his father died. Often the absence of a father or a mother would result in troubled behavior or illegal behavior such as substance abuse, or worse – suicide.

Also, teachers of these children can't recognize and deal with children who lost their dad, mom, or both. Children who lost a parent and looked different from everyone else could be one of those at risk for bullying.

I was thankful that Liam avoided being bullied mainly because of his friends. Ryo was a bully before, but he changed after he met Liam. He took Liam under his wing. Liam even made Ryo intervene when bigger kids or students were bullying small kids. Nobody else dared in bullying Liam. If they did, they would answer to Ryo. Emma, Ryo, and Liam have been inseparable. They would spend most summers together, and they became good friends.

Liam's 12th birthday was just around the corner. So, we decided to make it different this year. We planned an out-of-town trip with Liam's friends instead of throwing a party at home.

"We would not be having a party at home this year for my birthday." Liam talked to his friends, including Ryo and Emma, before his birthday.

"How come?!" Emma said with a worried look.

"Yeah, how come. I was so excited. What happened?" Ryo was visibly annoyed because he loved Liam's birthday parties every year. He always says that he has the best birthday parties.

My Little Shogun

"Change of plans. They are planning a trip and wanted me to celebrate it with you guys. So, guess where we will be going if you guys come?" Liam held back, and everyone was so quiet with anticipation.

"Come on, Liam. Tell us." Another friend of Liam chimed in.

"Super Nintendo World in Osaka. We will go there riding the Shinkansen (bullet train). Who is coming with me?" Liam saw his friends with wide eyes and momentarily could not speak. Then after a few seconds, everyone raised their hands.

"Wow!"

"I am in! I cannot wait to ask my mom and dad."

"You do not have to worry about anything. My mom and Sobo will take care of it. All you need to do is ask for permission from your parents. They can come, too, and we will all have a blast."

"Yahoooo! I cannot wait and ask Baba(grandma)!" Everyone was so excited to go home and ask for permission.

"You let me know tomorrow, OK." He waved goodbye to them as he headed to the train station to go home. Ryo and Emma would be with their sobo (grandma) and go somewhere else after class. So, they stayed behind and waited for her.

"See you tomorrow, Liam. Bye!" Emma shouted as he turned towards the local train station. Liam headed back home, where Kate was excited to know who would come to his birthday trip.

As Liam walked the Kyoto streets, he was not alone. Kenji was always on his side. Most kids would have imaginary friends until they were eight to nine years old, and some would extend into their teens. I knew that Kenji was important to Liam and assured him that it was OK even if he was the only one who saw Kenji. Liam and I had an agreement that whatever discussions he had with Kenji, he needed to keep it to himself and only share it with his Mama or Sobo. As he grew older, he understood why we wanted to keep it to ourselves even more. Liam realized that not all had a Kenji, and others might treat him differently. However, based on our conversations when he shared what they talked about, Kenji was a blessing.

I felt at that time that Liam was lucky to have a constant companion, a kami---guardian angel. An unexplained force or guardian angel that hovered around or walked beside him. Kenji has kept him company all these years and has his best interest at heart. No matter if Kenji were real or not, I would be eternally grateful for how Liam felt the support that he got from him.

"You are getting older musuko (son). I am so proud of you. You have grown into a caring young man. You are indeed your father's son." Kenji, who wore a dark blue kimono and a black hakama(trousers), talked to Liam as he walked side by side with him in the streets of Kyoto. They have walked this same path together more than a thousand times.

"Proud of me? You are pulling my leg. What do you want?" He knew what he meant but decided to joke around him a little.

"Liam, you are not fooling me. I see that smile in your eyes even if you try to keep a straight face. But, of course, I know you by now when you are "playing" me. I am just so proud of you, son. You have withstood the worst enemy a man could have."

"Who?!" Liam asked curiously.

"Himself…We are our worst enemies. Nobody can bring us down like our own self. Our selves could either uplift us or destroy us especially in unimaginable circumstances. You reminded me of myself when I was young. Do you remember the story that I told you about how I won the battle of Okehazama?"

"How could I not remember? You do not give me a chance to forget." He laughed teasingly.

"Did I already tell you about it?!! I will tell you again. I was outnumbered and ready to quit…." Kenji told the story again about his conquest. Liam just allowed Kenji to talk about himself again. He loved seeing him so animated and alive when he spoke about his past. Liam smiled as he listened to him.

"Great Story, Kenji!"

"I am glad you liked it again!" He made a booming laugh and was pleased with himself.

"I always look forward to talking to you, Kenji. But others might not see you or understand why I see you. They might even think I am foolish if I tell them I have an imaginary friend like you. They might call you a temporary phase of childhood. Some might even think I am crazy for seeing things they perceive as unreal. But whatever…" Liam makes two W signs with his fingers as he talks to Kenji.

"Real or not, it does not matter to me because you are important to me. You will be my friend forever." Liam said sincerely.

"I will be your most loyal friend too, Liam."

"Do you think that you will be with me forever?"

"I do not know Liam. I am happy that I am with you. You are like a son to me. I know I have a purpose in your life, and the one thing that I don't know is when I will finish serving that purpose. I know there is a limit to this. I do not know how long my penance is. I was given a chance by a higher power to make up for my past sins. Some higher force believed that I was worth saving. I do my penance by being a kami for the Gamo clan. I don't know how long I will do this."

"So, I am not the only one in my family tree that you followed?" Liam asked.

"Yes, but I don't exactly remember. All I remember is after following one of your ancestors; I go back in deep prayer. Then, I wait in darkness praying until my next penance of being pulled to a consciousness of a newborn in your lineage or clan."

"I wish I could end your penance."

"I wish you could. But, no worries, I already got used to it. Besides, I am thankful I did not go to that place where bad people go, which I don't want to describe.

"Uhuuhuhuhu...The thought of it sends shivers to my spine. But I know one thing. I hear a bell during my deep prayers. And when it ends, I get attached to another relative of yours when they are born. So, I think your time here on earth is different from where I pray. Time there is immaterial."

"Bell?!" Liam asked,

"I hear a bell in a Shinto temple before I get pulled out of my deep prayer. The end of the ringing signifies I am about to start or finish my penance."

"No matter how long you are with me. I am glad you are with me. Thank you!"

My Little Shogun

"I am, too! I love you, Liam." Kenji loved Liam like his own son.

Chapter 10
Missouri

LIAM

A bright reflected white light blinded me as I took a photograph of the Arch in St. Louis. I just came out of a path from one of the oldest churches in Missouri, The Basilica of Saint Louis, King of France. I spent most of my summer months visiting my grandparents in Chesterfield, Missouri. They took me everywhere – to places that you would not even expect existed in this place, such as big lakes filled with bass and trout and secluded resorts that value beauty and hospitality. Enchanted places where a mist would greet your early morning. It would remind you how much a serene place could warm your heart and give you peace of mind. It would make you realize what you have been missing your whole life.

Missouri is a beautiful place. It is a place where people still open doors for you. It is where the family came first. Where hard work, using your bare hands, tilled and shaped lands in every corner of the state was valued and much appreciated. People who visited would often find themselves not wanting to leave. So, they set their roots here and built their homestead.

My grandparents were no different. They fell in love with the charm of this place. They bought land and, bit by bit, transformed the land into beautiful landscapes with unending stretches of white fences. You could spend hours and hours just staring at how beautiful and peaceful the view is while seated on wooden chairs on your front porch. Time somewhat moved slowly here. It may be why people had enough time to be mindful and took pride in being kind to one another.

Grandfather Tristan came from a family of aviators. His father was a World War II veteran who flew North American p-51 mustangs across the Pacific Ocean. He grew up in a household where the conversations ranged from plane engines to flight plans. My grandfather eventually built his own chartered jet company from the ground up and has not stopped since expanding it. Even though he has been busy with his company, he still finds time to sit and talk to me on the front porch every morning. We spend a couple of hours just listening to early shows on the radio while talking about mostly anything under the sun.

"A few days from now, we will take you to Big Cedar." He sat beside me on a wooden chair, sipping a cup of black coffee.

"What are you drinking, Grandpa? It smells good."

"Oh this, it's brewed coffee that my friend gave me. He grounded Brazilian and Ethiopian beans then mixed them. Your grandma does not allow me to drink coffee with sugar and cream now. She said that would help me with my cholesterol and high blood pressure."

"Is that the reason why you take medications in the morning as well?"

"Oh, the three white pills I take in the morning. Yes, your grandma said I had to take them as advised by my doctor. If it were up to me, I would not be taking them. So, don't tell your grandma that I sometimes forget to take them."

"I will tell grandma." I grinned sheepishly.

"Nooooo. I will be in trouble." He complained.

"OK. I won't. Are you working today?"

"Yes, but it's the last day before the long weekend. And then we will have a great time at Fun Mountain in Big Cedar."

"I'll see you soon then, Grandpa!" I waved goodbye to him. He went inside the car as the driver pulled in front of the driveway.

"See you later." My grandfather waived back with his outstretched hand outside his car window. The car exited through the opened electrical gate and disappeared from my sight.

Those were some of my memories when I spent my summer vacations in the U.S. I was looking forward to seeing my grandparents again, and they were supposed to be coming in from Missouri to be with me on my 12th birthday trip to Super Nintendo World in Osaka, Japan.

Three nights before my birthday, my mom and I were with my sobo (grandma) and jiichan's(grandfather's) house while we prepared for our trip over the weekend.

"Five of your friends with parents are coming, right, Liam?" My mother was getting organized as she prepared to get tickets early for the trip and booked a place to stay.

"Yes, Mommy!" I stared at her laptop as she tried to double-check all the tickets for the trip and a villa she rented for the weekend.

"I got the shirts with Mario, Super Nintendo World logo printed on each."

I pulled one and saw the logo embossed on the shirt's right upper chest part, and I noticed jiichan added more text to it.

"Happy Birthday to the best grandson, Liam!"

I was surprised and felt so loved.

"Thank you, Jiichan," I said sincerely.

"Those look great, Otousan! Thank you so much." My mom momentarily looked up and got a glimpse of the shirts.

"Ring, ring, ring!" My mom's phone suddenly rang.

"Who is calling me tonight?!" Mom asked as she stood up and went to her phone, which was on top of a receiving table near the foyer-like place of the house.

It was Grandma Elizabeth who was calling. "Mom is calling?! Hello, Mom…"

I saw her standing near the table with her back slightly turned. Then, I heard incomprehensible words and momentary questions from my mom.

"What happened to Dad?" I overheard their conversation, and I started to be concerned about grandpa. My mom headed to an adjacent room and closed the door behind her. I don't remember how long they talked, but it seemed long. I waited for her to come out and tell us what happened.

She finally came out of the room and headed towards us, "My dad and mom can't come. Dad is in the emergency room. His blood pressure shot up to 220/110, and he was not feeling himself. Grandpa is OK now, and they gave him some medication to bring it down slowly. I think they are deciding if they need to admit him to the hospital or if he continues to be OK, they will send him home. I told them to let dad rest and not push on the trip to come here. He might need to rest and get better first."

"Ring, ring…"

"Hello, Mom?" She stopped talking as she listened what Grandma Elizabeth. She took the phone call in front of us.

"They will keep him overnight and place him on observation. They are worried that his stroke-like symptoms might come back. And Grandpa wants to talk to you, Liam."

"Hello, Grandpa! Are you OK?" I saw his face via facetime.

"I am alright. See, I can move everything, and Grandma is here with her whip to keep me straight. So, let us not talk about me. Instead, I wanted to say advanced Happy Birthday to you, my beautiful boy. I love you, son!"

"I love you too, Grandpa.…"

"I will stay here overnight, and I will see you soon when I get better, OK. I am so sorry if we could not come this year. We wanted to come, but Nana, Sam, and your mom are worried and wanted me to stay."

"It's OK, Grandpa."

"Have fun and send us pictures, OK.

"OK. We'll do that, Grandpa."

"Give the phone back to your mom. Love you to the moon and back, son.

"Mwah!" I gave my grandpa a flying kiss and gave the phone back to my mom.

Mom talked to him for a while and came back to continue getting tickets.

"Don't worry, Liam. Grandpa will be OK. He is from Missouri. He is tough as nails and will bounce back like a champ. So, let's continue making sure everything is OK for our upcoming trip. We will call him again the night before we ride the Shinkansen (bullet train)."

Grandpa Tristan was released the next day and canceled all his appointments for the whole week to rest at home. But, as mom promised, we called him the night before, and he was in high spirits. He told us to have fun and play some Mario games for him.

Early Saturday morning, we all met at the Kyoto station wearing our red Mario shirts, which Jiichan (Grandpa) bought under our light black jackets. We took the 8:00 AM scheduled time and sat on our reserved seats.

"I am so excited, Liam. Happy, Happy birthday to you. Here is my gift. I made that for you." I was seated next to Emma and Ryo. The trip would only last about 15 minutes, and you would hardly see places near the train because of how fast it moved.

"Thanks, Emma." I opened it and saw a red jewelry box with embossed letters on it.

"I helped put your name on the box, Liam. You are welcome." Ryo said while keeping a broad grin on his face.

"Thank you, Ryo and Emma. I like it." I thanked them even though I did not realize what I was supposed to put in it at first.

My Little Shogun

"You can place in there the necklace that your dad gave you so that you will always know where you placed it. I know that necklace is special to you and I...." Ryo interrupted Emi and pointed to himself to tell Emma to include him.

"Or we thought of giving you a special box to keep it in. So, you would not lose it." Finally, Emma finished what she was saying.

I did not realize how thoughtful they were, and now I had a place for my dad's necklace. I appreciated the gift. Emma and Ryo started talking about who did most of the work, and I could hear them from the background. Then, I suddenly heard Kenji's voice. He turned to me and started to talk. He rarely spoke to me when I was with someone, but he could not hold himself back this time.

"That's a beautiful box for your precious necklace. But, Liam, I knew the man who owned that metal fragment that you are wearing.

"His name is Gamo Ujisato. It's part of his armor. He saved my family. I am eternally grateful for what he did for my family. Don't speak to me. I know it's weird for you to talk to someone no one sees. I just wanted to let you know how happy I am that you took great care of it. The person who wore that was a great man. Thanks, Liam! And Happy Birthday, my son! I will shut up now. Sorry..." You could see from his face that he felt embarrassed that he interrupted my conversations with my friends.

"It is really fine... and I will take care of it." I looked at Kenji and waited for him to look me in the eye. When he turned his face towards me, I bowed towards him. His eyes were watery as he did the ojigi or bowed back at me.

My Little Shogun

"You were saying something, Liam?" As they saw me staring in the aisle with my head bowed.

"I said it's a special gift and I will take care of it. Thank you."

Emma turns to his brother, "See, I was right. He loved it." And we all giggled while Kenji kept a smile while looking at us.

We reached the Shin-Osaka station in no time and would use the Osaka inner loop JR lines to get to Universal City station, where the theme park was just a stone's throw away. The theme park was like one of the levels of the popular game, Super Mario Bros. game which was super-sized.

The Super Nintendo World was everything we envisioned it to be. I could not remember the last time I had so much fun with friends and family. We spent the night in a nearby hotel and went home the next day.

"Thanks, Liam. Happy, Happy Birthday! We will see you in school tomorrow." Emma waved goodbye as we all parted ways from the Kyoto station.

"Bye, Emma. Thanks, everyone." I waved back to Emi and all my friends. Then, we all crossed the adjacent street, and we headed back home.

Days turned to weeks, and it was mid-November when I saw the maple trees were in full shades of red, and some still had an orange hue. It was the perfect season to visit Kyoto when everything looked picturesque. The playful colors of the trees made our commute to school something to look forward to every day. I was not alone anymore. I have my friends, Ryo, and Emma, with me to share every moment. We became inseparable and spent almost every lunch break and after-school activity together.

My Little Shogun

My soba and mom were glad to see me happy. Finally, I have true friends.

Tourists have been steadily increasing in numbers. You could see them with maps on their hands as they tried to navigate the different trains; they needed to ride from point A to B.

"Excuse me. Can I ask for some directions?" A woman with a red hat who seemed to be an American asked us as we headed home.

Ryo and Emi were surprised and understood what she was asking but could not answer back quickly. They knew how but were shy because they were still learning how to speak English fluently.

"Do you know where Kyoto station is?" She asked again as she saw Ryo and Emma nod.

There were a few seconds of silence, and then I answered her question.

"You are almost there. It's just four blocks away. Take this street, and in the end, it will be on your right." I answered her question as if English was my native tongue.

"Your accent is perfect. Arigatou gozaimasu!" The woman tried to bow as she thanked us. And we bowed back.

"My friends and I all speak English. So, we are happy to help. And you are welcome!" I smiled, and I could see my friends swell with pride. It was the result of years of having a personal tutor at home.

We finally reached Emma and Ryo's house, where Emiko was already waiting for them.

"We are so proud of you, Liam. You should teach us."

"OK. But I know you could do it. You just need practice."

"See you tomorrow, Liam. Please say Hi to Mrs. Gamo." Ryo was now out of view, and all I could see was Emma, who stood still as she waited for me to head my way home.

"Take care, Liam. I will see you tomorrow." Emma said, smiling while waving goodbye.

"Bye, Emma." I started walking again in the streets by myself. I was almost near my home when I saw my mom. It was unusual for her to wait for me outside the house. I felt something was wrong. She looked distraught.

I hurried up and ran to her side. As I kissed her on the cheek, she whispered. "Something happened to Grandpa...."

"Nana just called, and Grandpa was not waking up. An ambulance is bringing Grandpa right now to the hospital. Let's go in and wait for them to call back. I am so sorry to surprise you with this news." My mom has tears in her eyes but tries to contain her panic inside. I felt that she was scared and needed someone to comfort her.

"Grandpa will be OK. Remember you said before he will bounce back like a champ. He will be OK." I hugged her tight, and we went into the waiting embrace of my grandparents. They were speechless and just wanted to be there for us.

We all sat in the living room while waiting for a phone call from Missouri.

"I told him not to drink too much Sake. Come on, old man, wake up..." Grandpa Hideshi talked to himself and paced back and forth the hall.

I could see Kenji, too. He was seated beside me and was silently praying for my grandpa.

"Hideshi, be still. And try to calm down." Sobo called out Grandpa Hideshi.

"It's OK, Mom. He is just worried like me. We will get answers soon. So, don't worry, Papa."

"Sorry, Kate. I am just worried. I'll try to settle down."

"Don't say sorry, Papa. It's alright. Any minute now, they...."

"Ring, ring, ring." My mom's phone rang as Sobo placed the wooden tray filled with green tea on the table.

"Hello, Mom! Are you in the emergency room now?" Grandpa Tristan was again in the emergency room, and a physician saw him. Nana and Sam were with dad, and they were at the bedside.

"A lot of people are around him now. They are trying to do all things at the same time. He is not fully responding when we call out his name, but I see him occasionally opening his eyes. He is hooked to a monitor now, and I don't understand what those red and blue numbers meant. One reads 130, the other reads 94. I see a blood pressure, and I think it's 190/110. The physician pushed hard on his sternum when he was not opening his eyes. He grimaced to pain, but his right hand and leg were the only thing that moved. Someone is drawing some blood. The doctor has not talked to us yet and was still examining dad." Nana talked to my mom over the phone as we waited for her to tell us what was happening.

"He is not waking up fully, Papa. The doctor is still examining him." Grandpa Hideshi stood up again and disappeared into the office. I felt he was worried sick about Grandpa Tristan and could not bear seeing him cry. He went into the study room.

"The doctor is coming. He might talk to us now. I'll ask him if I can put you on speakerphone." Nana continued to talk to Mom over the phone.

My mom put her on speakerphone, too. I could see my mom breathing fast, but she tried to maintain her composure while waiting for the doctor to speak.

"Mrs. Alberts?" I could hear the doctor asking Nana Elizabeth.

"Yes, I am his wife, and this is my daughter Sam, and my other daughter is on speakerphone. She lives overseas and would like to hear our conversation."

"I am Dr. Deepankar, an emergency room physician, and this is my colleague Dr. Dhaval, who is a neurologist. We will be taking care of your husband. We will be running some tests and imaging studies, such as a C.T. scan of the head on your husband. We are not exactly sure what's causing him not to respond fully, but we will make sure to rule him out for a stroke. We will give him some medication to bring his blood pressure down slowly.

"Time is of the essence here, and we need to move quickly to intervene if required. Do you have any questions for me at this moment before I leave you with Dr. Dhaval?"

"Please do all you can for him and just update us for any changes. Do you have any questions? Sam or Kate?" Nana Elizabeth asked.

"No, Mom." I heard my Auntie Sam over the phone

"I'll just wait for an update later. Can you call me back, Mom, when the results come in?"

"Yes, Kate. I'll call you back." The call ended.

"Here you go, Kate." My grandpa gave my mom a piece of paper with something written.

"Go to him. He needs you now. We will be OK here. We will take care of Liam while you are away." Grandpa reassured her.

"Oh… Otousan." My mom with tears in her eyes. She hugged grandpa tightly. He bought her an airplane ticket to leave tonight to be with Nana and grandpa in Missouri.

She turned towards me. Before she could utter a word, "I'll be OK, Mom. Hug Grandpa for us."

My Little Shogun

Chapter 11
Crossroad

GATES

"9:15 PM." The departure time was in bold black ink marked in the middle of the ticket bought by my father-in-law. I was seated near the departure gate before my boarding time at KIX (Kansai International) - Airport in Osaka, Japan. It was a 28- to-30-hour trip before arriving at STL (St. Louis-Lambert International) Airport.

It was a chilly mid-November. The maple trees' different shades of red were one of the main protagonists in this spectacular array of fall season colors. A lot of tourists and travelers were in the airport during this time. Families from different backgrounds flocked to see its majestic views. Some were trying to catch late flights to see nature's beauty as the sun rose the next day. While I was waiting for my flight, a young boy around five years old was staring at me. I bowed my head towards him and smiled. He then got up from his chair, carried his Teddy Bear, and walked towards me.

I did not want to stare at him, so I focused my attention on my iPad as I checked my email. As I read one of my emails, I noticed that he was standing three feet in front of me. He waved his little hand and patiently waited to get my attention.

"Hi! How are you?" I greeted the curious boy as I tucked a strand of hair away from my line of sight.

"What are you watching?"

"Oh… I am just checking some mail. Do you want to watch something on my tablet?" Without hesitation, I offered my iPad for him to use. I was taken aback by his confidence.

He held his chin as if thinking what to say next. "Let me ask my mom first. I'll be right back."

"*Smart boy.*" I smiled as he ran four rows of chairs to ask permission from his mom. His mom gave him a small red can, and he held it in his hands as he returned to sit beside me.

"My mom said it's OK. Is it OK to have a snack while I watch?"

"Of course." I was still amazed by his confidence that I forgot to introduce myself and ask for his name.

"What do you want to watch?"

"Can we watch Bluey?" He was seated next to me while he tried to open a red can of Pringles.

"Do you want me to open it for you?"

"Oh yes, please. Thank you." I grabbed it and placed the iPad on his right side. I pushed play and gave the red can back to him.

"Thank you. Here, have some of my Pringles." I smiled back at him and got a couple. For twenty minutes, we ate and watched Bluey together. After the last episode, he stood up. He was about to walk back to his mom, "Oh… Thank you again for letting me watch. I hope everything will be OK, Gates…."

"How did you know my name?" I was surprised.

"I read it in front of your tablet. It said, 'Property of my Gates.'" I felt a cold chill and was shocked. Hanzo gave this to me and placed a sticker with the name he fondly called me.

"I saw you were sad, and I wanted to cheer you up. You are smiling now. So, I have to go back to my mom."

"What is your name?" I asked him.

"I am Enzo. Thank you again. See you." His parents were walking towards us. They were about to board their plane at the gate next to mine.

"Thank you for your kindness." Enzo's mom reached out for my hand and bowed in front of me before they left for their boarding gate.

"Never did I feel nor experience something like that from a stranger. It reminded me of my husband's kindness with a simple gesture made by Enzo. There are many things in this world that you and I could not explain. Maybe my Hanzo was trying to comfort me through Enzo. Whatever force that allowed that happy moment with Enzo to happen, I will be forever grateful for the comfort he has given me in my time of need."

"Passengers of Flight 1182 with first-class tickets, you can proceed to the gate and begin the boarding process...." I suddenly heard the overhead announcement for my flight. I stood up and boarded my plane, which was outward bound to Missouri, U.S.A.

"Hello, Liam. I am already on the plane and about to leave in a few minutes. I'll call you when I land in St. Louis. Be good, OK…Listen to Grandma and Grandpa. I already miss you. Love you, Liam."

"I love you too, Mom."

My Little Shogun

The flight stewardess was making a hand gesture of putting the phone down as the plane was preparing to leave. "I'll have to hang up now. I'll talk to you soon. Bye, Liam…"

Barely awake, I hopped into Sam's car and headed out to the hospital.

"Coffee? I got you a hot Pumpkin Spice Latte." Sam grinned as she noticed my sleepy eyes. I looked like someone who had not slept for days. I was not able to get much rest on the airplane. I call it passenger-pilot sickness. I flew in planes more as a pilot than being one of the passengers.

"Thanks, Sam." I opened the lid and smelled its aroma before I took a sip. I was like a little kid holding the cup with my two hands as I enjoyed every sip of my coffee.

"We rode out of the airport towards the direction where the sun shined brightly on our faces. Not much has changed since I was here two years ago. Along the highway, I got a glimpse of the Gateway Arch. It gives me a warm, comforting feeling every time I see it. A sensation as if someone was hugging me for the first time after we had not seen each other for a long time. I have seen it from flying planes with my dad to celebrating special holidays with my family underneath it.

The Gateway Arch holds a special place in my heart and our family. There is even an old church beside it where my parents got married. So, it has been pretty much a constant companion throughout our lives. It's forever present, and you can always count on it to be there for you if you want to see it. All you need to do is seek it out, and it will give back the sentimental feelings you yearn for. It would remind you of things you have forgotten and important persons you've been missing. I miss my dad, and I hope he will be OK…."

My Little Shogun

We pulled into the covered parking lot and headed to the third floor, where the stroke unit was. The hospital was busy, and I recognized a familiar scent, a mixture of coffee and cleaning products. It brought back memories of visiting my sister when she was still young. She would be in and out of the hospital due to frequent asthma attacks.

As Sam and I were about to open Dad's room, a nurse was about to come in.

"Hi, I am Jodie, Mr. Alberts' nurse. You are Kate, right?" The nurse held the door handle as she gave me a huge smile. You could tell that she knew me and was expecting me.

"Yes," I replied.

"I heard so many things about you. Your mom is inside with your dad. He is having a better day today. He has been waiting for you."

She opened the door, and I saw Mom holding Dad's hand. He was trying to talk to Mom but was slow about it.

"Good morning, Sir! Look who I found in the hallway." Jodie knew that the sight of me would make his day. He saw me from afar and raised his left hand towards me. Tears began falling as I ran towards his embrace.

"Hi, Dad." He hesitated to speak. He was embarrassed to let me know that his words now were slurred and would not come out the way he wanted. He could understand what I said, but he could not express himself well yet.

"Aii…" He forced a word and tried to kiss my cheek as I saw a tear roll out from his right eye.

"Don't cry, Dad. I am here now. We are here. Let's get better together, OK?" I hugged him tighter.

Mom explained that after they gave him medicine in the middle of the night, he suddenly woke up. He has been trying to speak since this morning. At first, he was frustrated, but he became calmer after the neurologist explained what had happened to him. He had a stroke caused by an irregular heart rhythm called atrial fibrillation. The left side of his brain was affected, including the part which made speech possible. He could understand what you and I were saying, but he could not express himself well enough. He had weakness in his right arm and leg but could move them slightly.

"The neurologist said that his blood pressure and labs this morning were within normal range. How he progresses or gets better depends on how his body recovers with the help of medications, including a blood thinner, which he needs to continue to take later. While we wait for him to show progress and improvement, he might need to go to an acute rehabilitation center for stroke patients." Mom tried to repeat what the doctor said.

"Daats Rye (That's right)!" Dad tried to confirm what my mom said. His fighting spirit was in full gear again, and he showed courage despite his fear of not knowing if he would get better or not.

"I see you have your quick wit back. I'll be here with you every step of the way, Dad." It was a gift to see my dad somewhat himself again.

"I thought I was going to lose my father. I thought I would have to relive those moments again of emptiness when Hanzo died. I had to crawl out of my despair, to be whole and be myself

again. I thank you, God, for putting a pause on taking my father to be by your side. Thank you for letting me have more time with him here on earth."

We took turns to be with Dad. My sister Sam would go first and stay with him if he needed help. We never left his side.

One Sunday morning, while Sam was with Dad, Mom and I sat on rocking chairs in front of the house where I grew up. There was a low mist that enveloped the fields and white fences. The view is enough to calm any restless soul that sees it.

"Thanks, Kate, for coming! We didn't expect you to hop in a plane and come so quickly." My mom said.

"The night we were on the phone talking about Dad, Otousan bought the ticket for me. He wanted me to be with Dad as soon as possible. Liam wanted me to go as well."

"Liam is a young man now. In a few more years, he will be in high school. Remember when I would wake up early in the morning during the weekend when I was in middle school to ride my horse and spend hours horseback riding. Dad would come out, too, and ride his horse with me. Together we took the trail out back and talked about almost anything. This house is special. I have a lot of memories of it. It's still beautiful, and it looked as I remembered it before I left to join the U.S. Air Force."

"I worry about you guys as I live across the Pacific. Who is going to take care of you and Dad?"

"Dad is doing better now, and we will be fine. Sam will be here. Just concentrate on Liam and continue to raise him right. You, being here when your dad needed you the most, is more than enough. Don't worry about us." Mom tried to reassure me even though I knew she was worried about what would come next since my dad could not run this farm and our business the way he used to.

"I know you guys can handle it, but I still worry."

"We will be alright, Kate. We bought this place because it was so peaceful, especially in the morning. You would not find this view in between the skyscrapers in the city. Look how the white paint in the fences remained untarnished. With this mist, it seemed that we had unending white fences." My mom was trying to change the topic. She did not want to be a burden.

"Is it your turn to sit with Dad tomorrow in rehab? He has been there for almost two weeks now."

"Yes, it's my turn. I will get dad some pancit and lumpia in a local international store nearby. I remembered he likes that a lot." I let her change the topic and remembered switching with Sam tomorrow. Sam was going back to work tomorrow as she was now a senior partner in the immigration firm where she started.

"Oh yes. It has been a while since dad ate that. That would be a pleasant surprise." Mom and I finished our coffee while reminiscing about things we did during my childhood.

It was 8:00 AM when I saw Sam in the lobby. We sat down for breakfast before she went to her office, only a few blocks away from the hospital.

"You look beautiful and very professional, Sam." I smiled as I noticed she wore her favorite dark blue pencil skirt suit with a white silk undershirt.

"What? This? I have four pairs of these with different shades of blue." She said, grinning.

"How was Dad?"

"You know that he is feeling much better when you see the physical therapist chasing him down the hallway. He will go home soon, and he can continue therapy at home. Speech is better. He would mess up a word or two but better than when he came in." My sister said while staring at me and knew I was thinking of something else.

"Did you sleep well last night?" Sam noticed I was not paying attention to her.

"Yes, I did. Why?"

"You have that look when you are bothered with something. For example, when you are worried, you bite your lip and place your hand on your chin."

"Oh, nothing. I was just worried about dad."

"Don't worry, he is doing much better now, and in a few days, he will be ready to go home.

"Beep. Beep." Sam's pager suddenly went off.

"Oh, look at the time. I must go, or I will be late for my date. I am sorry for my early meeting." She made a soft chuckle.

"No worries. Mom and I will see you later. Bye." Sam smiled and left me at the cafeteria. I sat there for a while as I thought of what to do next.

"I feel that they need me here now more than ever, but I don't know if Liam would agree to come here to the U.S. He would miss his friends, his Sobo, and Grandpa Hideshi. I worry that he will have to start all over again if he transfers to a local school here. He already has friends there, and I don't know what

My Little Shogun

the change would do to him. Okaasan and Otousan would miss him too. I just don't know what to do.

Hail Mary, full of grace....Please pray for me to make the right choice. Amen."

I headed to my dad's empty room. He was not there. Jodie saw me and said Dad would be right back. He was finishing up with his therapy in the gym. I sat in his room and waited for him to return. As I sat beside his bed, I noticed he had pictures of us near the window. He asked Mom to bring them from home. He has his favorite picture near his bed. It was a picture of dad and me riding horses when I was young. I held it in my hands and remembered that day when we were all together enjoying a beautiful day. I was standing near his bed when I heard his laughter. He was a few meters from his room. I put back the picture and turned towards the door.

"You are doing so well, Mr. Alberts. You have great strength in your arms, and you can use your four-point walker with ease. You still need to be careful because you somewhat drag your right foot and internally rotate it when you step forward. But, otherwise, I did not expect how fast you could recover. I feel that they will be preparing for your discharge soon. Besides, you have such a supportive family at home." Ben, one of the physical therapists, encouraged my dad.

I could see him now. He looked so happy as he turned his walker to enter his room.

"Hi, Kate! You herrre. Thiz Bennn. He helpzz me a lot. Ben, thiz my daughter Kate." He was missing and mispronouncing some words, but he was better. He has been working hard with the speech therapist too.

"Hi, Dad! Nice to meet you, Ben. Thank you for helping Dad. Do you want to sit here for a while, Dad?"

"Yezz, I would love to, zzo that I can feel the zzun in my face." I sat beside him, and he could not stop staring at me. He was so happy to see me again even though I visited him yesterday.

"Stop staring at me, Dad.…"

"I'm zzorrry. I am juzzt happy to zzee you."

"I am just kidding. It's OK. I was just messing with you. I heard that the doctor was planning to discharge you soon."

"My doctor zaid I might be rrready tomorrrow. I zzpoke with Liam lazt night. He called…. we talked. I mizz being arrround him. And I feel that you will mizz him too. Why don't you go back to him? I am getting betterrr…. will be going home zzoon. We'll be fine. He needzz his mom to be therrre." I was surprised by what my dad said. He thought more about Liam and me than himself despite what happened to him. That's how my dad is. He would place others first and often forget about his needs and wants.

"I know you and mom will be OK. Sam will always be here for you. But I was thinking about being here for you, too."

"Don't worrry. We will zzell buzzinezz and planez."

"Is that what you want, Dad?"

"No, but I will be finnne with it." Dad looked away and avoided eye contact with me. He seemed teary-eyed.

"Is it OK if you hold off on selling it? What if I take over the business? Let me talk to Liam first."

My Little Shogun

"OK. Talk to Liam if he agrrreezz. You take overrr. If he doezz not, then I'll zzell. Let him decide without being prezzured. What everrr hizz decizzion, I will be OK with it."

"Ok, dad. I'll talk to him."

We sat in his room and talked more, while watching T.V. together.

"Christmas advertisements are now being played. It is now the first week of December. Christmas decorations are now on full display in local stores and public places. Santa's Magical Kingdom lights in Eureka, Missouri, are now lit. You could watch the commercials with Christmas songs and Christmas movies on T.V. now. I remember as a child, my dad and mom made sure that we had the most fun and built heartfelt memories during this season. I suddenly thought of Liam and how I miss him.... I must get back to him. I need to get back to Kyoto, Japan."

Dad was eventually discharged from the hospital with outpatient therapy and personal caregivers at home if needed. My mom and sister were adjusting quite well to Dad's needs. He has a scheduled routine. Mom momentarily managed the business with Sam's help. Finally, it was time for me to go back home to Liam. I caught the early flight home and rode the Shinkansen (bullet train) from Osaka to Kyoto. I did not tell Liam that I was coming home that day. I wanted to surprise him.

It was a cold evening in Kyoto. People already wore their winter clothes. As I stepped out of the Shinkansen, I noticed the transformation of Kyoto station into an orchestra of lights moving in unison and to the beat of old familiar Christmas songs. If you are looking for the best place in Japan to feel a little Christmas cheer, Kyoto station is the place to be.

My Little Shogun

They were playing "Silent Night" in their public address (P.A.) system, while in the middle of its great hall stood a gigantic tree adorned with bright lights of red, yellow, and green dancing with every beat of the song. Behind it was the grand station staircase converted into a sea of lights that had animated Christmas gifts displayed as being dropped from above.

The whole great hall was a spectacular display of technology trying to capture the spirit of Christmas. It brought a smile and cheer to everyone who saw it. Every smile you see on each face is a constant reminder that despite what was happening in the world, goodness still exists and will forever be no matter what happens.

I arrived at Otousan and Okaasan's house, where Liam was staying. It was dark outside with lights upfront unusually turned off. It was only 7:00 PM, and it was too early for them to be sleeping. Maybe they ate out together on this Friday night. Oh well, I have keys and would just wait for them. I would surprise them when they come home. With the help of dimmed streetlights, I noticed that their door had a green wreath hanging in front of it with red and gold ornaments. I had difficulty opening the door as I inserted my key in the slot. I had to put the bag of gifts down and use the flashlight app on my phone to help me open it.

"That's weird. The door is not locked...." I turned the doorknob and walked in.

"Suurrpprrrise!!!" They turned on the lights, and everyone was there. I saw Liam holding a sign that said, "Welcome home, Mom! We love you."

My dad spilled the bean to organize a surprise welcome party for me. A seven-foot Christmas tree towered in the room. It had giant red ornaments and red ribbons like the tree in the Kyoto station.

"Wow…That's why it was so dark outside. I was supposed to be the one to surprise you." Everyone laughed. "Thank you so much for this. It's the season of happiness and sharing. Let's eat! Thanks again, everyone. You all made this night special." As I finished talking to the crowd, Liam hugged and kissed my cheek.

"Welcome home, Mom!" He said happily. I could see the joy in his eyes.

"You stinker. Grandpa told you that I was coming home, right?"

"Yes, he did. He wanted to do something special for you when you came home. That's why he called us so that we could prepare. I am so happy you're here. I thought you were going to miss celebrating Christmas with us."

"Nah, me? Never. Of all the places in the world that I could be right now, I would rather be where my Liam is."

"Thanks, Mom." Then, he gave me a warm embrace again.

"Let's eat!" I hugged Otousan and Okaasan. I could not thank them enough for what they have done for Liam and me.

When everyone left, Okaasan and I were left trying to clean and tidy things up.

"I am glad you arrived home safe. We talked to Tristan, and he is making good progress with his recovery. Liam was so excited to know you were coming home. He helped so much in making sure that you had the best surprise party ever."

"Thank you so much. And thank you for taking care of Liam while I was away."

"You are welcome, Kate. You look sad. Is something bothering you?" Okaasan noticed I was spacing out and staring at the corner of the table.

"I have to be honest with you, Okaasan. I am worried about my dad. A bigger part of me wants Liam to stay here, and a part of me wants to be there for my dad. I want to be there for them. But I would also miss you and Papa Hideshi."

"My child, no matter where you go, you will never lose us. You are our daughter and will always be. You do what you think is right, and we will support you all the way."

"Thank you." What she said meant a lot to me, more than she would ever know. I have always treated her like my mom.

"Did you tell Liam yet?" She asked.

"I was thinking about that, too. But I don't know when the right time is to tell Liam. My dad was hesitant to ask for help because he knew it would affect Liam. But he said whatever Liam's decision would be, he will support it wholeheartedly."

"Liam is smart, and I trust him to make the right decision for himself. You say that he is his father's son. But I believe that he is actually and truly his mother's son. So, be honest with him and let the chips fall wherever they may. Don't worry about Papa and me. We will be fine. You do what you think is right...." I hugged Okaasan like I would hug my mother, who means the world to me.

Liam was in his room watching again the videos that Hanzo gave him. He was unaware of the conversations Okaasan, and I was having.

My Little Shogun

"I am proud of you, son. Happy Happy 12th Birthday! And I am pretty sure that you are doing great in school and taking care of Mom. Don't tell her this, but Mom is always right.... On your 12th Birthday, I would like to talk about something different and uncomfortable, bullying.

Remember when you were young, you came home sad. We talked about the kid who pushed you, and we both learned something that day. We learned that you need not endure any form of bullying. It would be best if you did not keep it to yourself, but instead talk to your friends and parents who care deeply about you and could make sure it stops.

To say you could erase bullying from existence is an illusion. Bullying will forever be present in our society. But to leave it to get worse and be left unchecked would be the most tragic of all things. It would be even worse when the few who believe it needs to end stop fighting or standing for the weak. You should never let this happen. Instead, continue to find ways to be strong for yourself and others.

Embrace being different. Have confidence in who you are. You will make mistakes but learn from them. And when you are strong, please don't forget the weak ones, OK? Love you. We will talk more about bullying after we celebrate your 12th birthday. Happy, Happy birthday again, son. I can't wait to celebrate it with you." Hanzo made these videos, not knowing he would be gone when Liam saw them. Later, Liam would tell me that Kenji, who I considered his imaginary friend, was watching it with him.

"I think your dad has a point with bullies. Back in my time when there were bullies, we just went to war and punished them." Kenji took his long sword out and imagined attacking his enemies

My Little Shogun

"But I think your dad's explanation and instructions are better than mine. You should listen to him. Your dad loves you a lot. I wish I knew how that felt. I never had a chance to be just a kid. I quickly had to learn to be an adult when I was supposed to be playing with toys. His idea sounds much better than mine."

"I love you, Kenji."

"I know you do, and I will go to the ends of the earth just for you."

"Tok, tok, tok." I knocked on Liam's door, and I heard him quickly closing his treasure trunk. I waited for him to say it was OK for me to come in.

"It's unlocked. You can come in now."

"Hey, Liam. Ready for bed? Were you watching one of Dad's videos?" I see Liam seated in front of his red trunk.

"Yes, I was. Dad was teaching me about bullies."

"That's a good one. Is anyone bullying you in school?"

"Nah. They would not dare. Ryo will crash them. I have the biggest bully as a friend."

"But Ryo has changed now and became good because of you."

"I guess." Liam smiled.

"I have to tell you something, Liam. I know that there is no better time to say it than now. I wanted to be honest with you, and I would like to know what you think about it, too."

"What is it about, Mom?"

"I was hoping to know what you think if we move to the U.S. and be with Grandpa and Nana over there. Grandpa needs our help."

"What did Grandpa say about me?" I was surprised that he knew that my dad would be thinking about what he thought.

"He would like to know what you thought about it and values whatever you say. There is no right or wrong answer here. He just wanted to know what you think about moving closer to him and leaving your friends, Soba, and Grandpa Hideshi, here."

"It would be really sad to leave my friends, especially Soba and Grandpa. He needs us, ha?" He asked. But it was more of a statement.

"They can manage if we don't come there. Auntie Sam will be there to help in some way or the other. So, do you want to stay here in Japan?"

"Hmmm. Grandpa Tristan needs us. I will miss my friends and Soba here. Hmmm. Even if grandpa needs us, he will not force that on us. He would like us to decide ourselves and do the right thing for us. I want Daddy to be proud of me, and I want to think beyond my own needs and wants. If you want to move to the U.S. and help Grandpa, I will be OK with it."

"Thank you, Liam. Love you."

"Love you to the moon and back, Mom."

We did not even realize that we embraced at the stroke of midnight.

Chapter 12
Bully

LIAM

"***D****inggg, dinggg.*" Somebody was striking a bell in a Shinto temple. I could hear it as I passed by on my way home alone. Emma and Ryo went with their soba and visited a nearby relative.

"*Dinggg, dinggg.*" The bell tolls again. People, mostly tourists, shell out money just to get a chance to strike it with an elongated wood tied to a steel rope chain attached to the ceiling of the shrine that housed the bell.

It was two days before school would end. I was walking home with Kenji by my side.

"The sound of that bell sends shivers to my inner core again. I don't know if it rings for me or someone else…. I feel my body shaking as if being sucked into it every time it's struck. Remember when I told you about my penance for all the bad things I did? Every time the bell tolls, it gives me a flashback of being surrounded by darkness where I prayed until I was pulled out of purgatory into the consciousness of your distant relatives or probably one of your descendants later. I had been doing it for a long time. I don't even know how many relatives I had been with from your line.

"One of your ancestors saved my family once in the past. A greater power, who I could not comprehend or even would not

attempt to understand, decided I was worth saving. In my consciousness, I must fulfill a purpose in your ancestors' or descendants' lives to save my soul. This purpose or effort is equal to or greater than the debt I owe to one of your ancestors who saved my family from certain death in the hands of my enemies."

"If I could say to that greater power, you already had made a difference in my life to end your penance…I will. I can't even begin to imagine how my life could have been without you by my side, especially when my dad died. Thank you for standing by me. I am so sorry that I became an obligation to you to fulfill your penance. If I had the power, I would end it."

"My son…I don't feel that you are an obligation. If it meant to do this penance until the end of time in exchange for your happiness, I would do it willingly and without contestation. I should be the one to apologize…."

"Apologize for what?"

"That you see me when others can't. I could not even put myself in your shoes when others think you are crazy to see and talk about somebody they could not see. It just does not make sense. And I am not even worthy of anybody's time and attention. Even me, I would think you are crazy. And dismiss what you see. I am so sorry to be a burden to you. Please forgive me."

"No one could explain most things in this world anyway. It's human nature to hide behind a blanket of explanations. Use theories to explain what we could not see and understand. To feel that we know everything tames our fears and aggression. Not knowing something, either true or false, would create chaos."

"You are wise beyond your years, my son. But remember, life will always challenge you, especially when you feel that you have a good understanding of it."

"Yes, Kenji. I will remember that, and I will never stop learning. Besides, I have you to guide me."

"Oh yes. I will be here. Speaking of changes, you will be leaving Japan and starting a new life in the U.S. with your mom in a month. Are you ready? I know I am. I am coming with you. I only have a little baggage."

"What baggage?"

"Me. I am your baggage. Makes sense? I made a funny joke." He laughed out loud with his joke.

"Where are you getting these jokes from?" I shook my head in disbelief at Kenji's joke and smiled back at him as he tried to make me laugh. We finally made it home, and Mom was waving at us. She stood where she always was while she waited for our return.

The day has come. We had four extra-large roller bags and two carry-ons each. We might have large loads, but our bags would look small compared to the vast friendship, love, and memories we were leaving behind.

"Do you have everything, Liam? How about the things in your treasure chest? Your dad's videos?" Grandpa Hideshi had a huge grin as if he knew a secret that I had kept all these years.

"How do you know about the videos, Grandpa?"

"Your dad used my very first iPad to make those videos. I helped him make them. Your dad loves you, and he was always thinking about you when he was alive.

"We would often talk about you. Your dad would often ask me questions about taking care and raising you the right way.

My Little Shogun

But he kept on asking if he was doing a good job. He did not want to fail you."

"Fail me, Grandpa?

"He did not want to fail in raising a good man. But unfortunately, I think he failed...."

"Oh. Yes, grandpa, I still have much to learn."

"He "failed" in thinking that he was just raising a good man. But little did he know, he went beyond his expectations. He raised a young man who would be great both in mind and spirit. I would miss you terribly, Liam. Call us once in a while, and let's talk. OK?" My grandpa then kissed my forehead and hugged me tightly.

"Love you, Grandpa," I said and hugged him back.

"Are you ready, Liam? Mom is all set. She is loading the bags in the car." My soba came in and saw Grandpa wiping a tear.

"Why are you crying, old man? He will be back." Soba winked at me.

"I am not. I just had something in my eye. Come on, Liam, let me help with your bags. Emma and Ryo are coming, too, to say goodbye." So, Grandpa Hideshi rolled my bags to the car, and we went our way to the airport with Ryo and Emma in the car with us.

"Do you know which middle school you are attending?" Ryo tapped me on my shoulder as he was riding in the back of the car with my mom. Emma was by my side.

"There are several schools in our district, and Mom already talked to them. We will meet with them once we get settled there in Chesterfield, Missouri."

"Don't forget us, OK?" Ryo said.

"I won't." Emma was silent as she held an envelope. She seemed sad and was avoiding eye contact.

"Are you OK, Em?" I asked her.

"I am OK, Liam…I am just sad that you are leaving."

"I am sorry, Emma. I'll try to stay in touch. I will miss you both, especially you." She was silent and did not answer. I let her be and did not want to upset her further. I saw her wipe something from the side of her face, but I did not dare to ask what it was nor tried to look at her.

"Goodbye, Grandpa and Grandma. I'll talk to you later and call you when we get to Grandpa Tristan's house. Can I hug you both?" They both kneeled in front of me, and I hugged them. My mom knelt too and hugged us all. I extended my right arm outward and called for Emma and Ryo to join in. We were all there on the floor for several seconds, with no one wanting to let go.

Finally, we stood up, and I was about to enter the security gates when Emma handed me the white envelope.

"I wrote you a letter Liam last night. Stay in touch, OK. We will miss you." She then held my hand for the first time. I held her hand, too, and did not want to let go.

"Bye, Liam."

"Bye, Emma." I waved goodbye as we entered the security gates and headed down the hallway towards our flight.

"My Dearest Liam,

My Little Shogun

Remember the time when we first met? You were reading "The Alchemist." I thought back then that was it, and you will be an acquaintance. But you proved to be much more than that, and you became a true friend to Ryo and me. We will cherish the time we spent together, the countless walks home together, the jokes we shared, and the kindness you have shown to us every day. I will miss you, friend. So, don't forget us, OK? Keep in touch. We might have an ocean between us, but we will be here for you no matter what.

P.S. I still have the "The Alchemist" book, and I am not giving it back. You come back here and get it back yourself if you want it. Bye=)

Emma"

I read her letter mid-flight, and I could not help smiling. I would really miss my friends. I felt that I would yearn for their presence and kindness as I was sure to meet challenges in my stay in the U.S.

It was the end of the first week of August when we arrived in Chesterfield, Missouri, two more weeks before school. Mom and Nana were able to prepare everything for me not to have a hard time transitioning to my new school. I would turn 13 years old this year, and I was just right to start seventh grade in middle school.

Grandpa Tristan was doing great with his speech and physical therapies. Nana even had time to renovate a room just for me and filled it up with my favorite things and posters I liked. It faced an open field that was fenced where horses could be carefree. From my window, you could see the green manicured grass fields. Its green color did not even fade even in the heat of summer. That view was one of my favorite places to stay, where

My Little Shogun

I would write and talk to my friends in Japan when I had the chance.

Mom started taking over the company the week we settled in. We were able to secure the middle school that I would be attending. Grandpa and Nana were so happy that we chose to be here and how quickly mom took over Grandpa's company of chartered jets. She even had clients who asked for her specifically to fly them worldwide. She would not normally do this for anyone, but she did it because he was a family friend, and it was for a special occasion.

"Can we schedule it for the 24th of August?" Dr. Desmond E. Dinaire, a well-known neurosurgeon in the St. Louis area, called in to book a flight. He is going to propose to his girlfriend, Clarice.

"Everything is set for that day. I have the ring, and a farmer, north of Branson, agreed to carve: **'BE MY CO-PILOT. WILL YOU MARRY ME?'** in his cornfield."

"Can I call you back? I would check something in our calendar."

"Yes, sure." Desmond was worried that he would not go ahead with his plans. My mom hesitated. August 24 was my first day in school. She wanted to be there for me. Mom checked prior flight plans that day and found the schedule full. She saw one plane was not scheduled yet, but it was Grandpa's favorite. No one uses that except him. So, she had to call him to ask permission. Mom called Grandpa, and she was surprised he readily agreed.

Mom called Desmond back. "We're booked for that week, but I have one special plane available. It's my dad's favorite, the

Cirrus Vision jet. Unfortunately, I will not be able to do it on the 24th, but can I do it on the 25th? Would that be, OK?"

"Yes, I'll take it. Thank you so much, Kate. It means a lot to me." Desmond was happy and nervous at the same time.

"Goodluck! I'll see you on the 25th of August around 10 AM after I drop off Liam."

"See you then. Bye." Desmond then hung up.

My first day in school finally arrived. Like me, Kenji was excited and anxious at the same time.

"Try not to be different, OK. Be yourself. Don't attract any attention to yourself. Ignore me, OK?!" Kenji was bubbling words that I could not keep up with and understand. I finally rolled my eyes on him and made gestures on both my hands to calm down.

"Excited for your first day in school?" Mom was driving, and I had a booster seat underneath me. I am almost 56 inches tall, and I will not need it next year.

"I am not used to this booster seat."

"Maybe next year you might not need that. You're almost 4'9" tall, and you can't be too careful."

"OK, mom."

"Do you want me to drop you off away from the school door so that they would not see me?"

"I don't mind them seeing you, Mom. It does not bother me. I want them to see my mom." My mom's eyes lit up, and she was proud of me for not being ashamed of being dropped off by her.

"Just for today. I'll pick you up around 3:30 PM. Tomorrow, you'll start riding the school bus. Thanks, Liam, for letting me be a mom."

"You are welcome, Mom." So, I went down our black H3 Hummer and gave my mom a flying kiss. My mom stayed for a little while until she could no longer see my black Star Wars bag as I entered the school's red double door.

"Here goes nothing. Be cool, Liam." I was trying to calm myself down.

"Yes, be cool. Be cool." Kenji anxiously echoed what I said. Red lockers lined the hallways, filled with students in between them. You could see a sea of different shades of brown, red, and dark yellow hair mixed in the crowd like you would see in a beautiful abstract painting. I, with my jet-black hair and bright blue eyes, stood up like a sore thumb. Some teenagers talked while they walked in groups, and some walked alone, quiet with their heads bowed down. The hallways were bigger than in Japan and much more crowded. There was a gathering of taller and older boys around a petite boy in the corner of the hallway. I saw the biggest one wearing a white shirt and jeans, taking something from the boy and telling him to be quiet.

I was about to head in their direction and see what all the fuss was about when I accidentally stepped on something soft.

I tapped the shoulder of the girl who was ahead of me. "Excuse me. You dropped this." I handed the blue ribbon to her.

"Thank you. What's your name?" She asked.

"Liam."

"I'm Taylor, by the way."

My Little Shogun

"Your English and accent are perfect. Where are you from?" One of the girls who was with Taylor asked curiously.

Before I had the chance to answer it, "You have such beautiful piercing blue eyes with long eyelashes." Interrupted by another girl in the group.

I was about to thank them when I got shouldered from behind. Then, I saw this taller kid pass me by on my left shoulder. He had a muscular build and was about seven inches taller than me.

"Is he bothering you, sis?" Taylor's brother said with a mean tone. His name is Bryce, and he is already in eighth grade. He is taller than most teenagers his age. Bryce and Taylor were initially from Palm Springs, California, and recently moved to Missouri last year.

"No, he was just returning my ribbon," Taylor replied to his brother.

I got distracted by Kenji as he tried to use his body to shield me from Bryce. But, to my surprise, Bryce's face was suddenly several inches in front of mine.

"Stay away from my sister. Don't ever talk to her again or else…." I could feel the anger in Bryce's voice as specks of his saliva showered all over my face. Everything happened so quickly that I did not feel his shoulder deliberately bump into mine. No one dared to intervene or say something. All were just standing and looking at us. There were several seconds of silence before everyone else started hurrying up to their classrooms. Students who witnessed it went about their business as if nothing happened.

My Little Shogun

I froze for a minute and did not hear any sound except for the breaths that I took. Kenji tried to talk to me, but I did not listen to him right away.

"I am so sorry, Liam. I am so useless, and I was not able to defend you. That boy was rude and disrespectful. But please snap out of it. Son.... don't let him ruin your day. Don't be late on your first day of school. Find your classroom fast before the teacher sees you alone in the hallway."

Kenji urged me to brush it off for a moment and focus on what was in front of me. There were only a few students left in the hallway, and I did not realize that Taylor glanced back at me without saying any word as she was whisked away by her brother.

"One foot after the other, Liam. That's it." I was encouraging myself as I tried to find my classroom. My heart dropped as I saw Taylor and her friends were my classmates. They turned their backs and did not dare to look at me. I saw an empty seat in the middle of the room and walked towards it.

"This seat is taken." He placed his bag on the chair and claimed the space as his property. I did not say a word. Instead, I moved to another empty seat in the corner of the room. Everyone was chatting with their seatmate. They probably have known each other for a long time.

"Did you see the picture I sent to you on Snapchat?" Said the boy with freckles on the bridge of his nose.

"Yeah, I saw it. Such a loser. I'll…" Their conversation was interrupted when the seventh-grade teacher walked into the room.

My Little Shogun

"Good morning, class. I am Mrs. Gross. We have a lot of new students. We'll start with quick introductions so that we will call each other by our names."

Everyone started to introduce themselves. Despite the painful start, I did it confidently and without any hesitation. But unfortunately, my confidence did not reflect the mixture of anger and sadness that my young mind was trying to sort out.

I did not know if my afternoon would be any different or worse than the morning that I had. But everything felt like dominos that once the first block began to fall, the rest would follow. When lunchtime came, everyone was busy catching up with friends while eating together at round tables. No one was seated alone except for me. Nobody wanted to sit with the new kid in school.

"Can I sit with you?" The school principal asked to sit with me when he noticed I was eating alone and barely touched my lunch.

"How was your first day in school? Made friends yet? I am Mr. Davis, by the way." He said, smiling.

"I'm Liam. Nice to meet you, Mr. Davis. It's OK so far. Not yet, but I'll make friends soon. It would just take some time. Thanks for asking, Sir."

"That's the spirit. You can always come to me if you have any problems, OK?" I did not say how Bryce welcomed me this morning. I decided not to start my first day as a snitch, even though I felt like a pariah after that encounter.

3:30 PM could not come any sooner. It felt like an eternity until that day ended. I felt relieved as I saw the black H3 Hummer drive through the elevated semi-circled pickup driveway.

"How was your first day in school? Did you make new friends?" Mom was smiling when she looked at me through the rear-view mirror. She anxiously waited to hear how my day was. Thinking of it now, it was a mistake not to tell her about what happened. But I did not want to get her worried.

"It was OK, Mom. I met the school principal, Mr. Davis. He was nice. How was your day?" I tried to change the topic.

"Really?! That's good to hear. But have you made friends yet?" She was persistent and sounded very excited.

"Not yet. Mom, but I will. It's just my first day." I forced a smile to hide the sadness in my eyes.

"I know everything is new and It's a big change from your old school. But we are always here for you no matter what. We will get through this together. Nana and Grandpa are waiting for us. Are you hungry? We'll eat out tonight."

"I'm starving. Are we going to eat out in Yayas?" I said excitedly. Suddenly, I heard my stomach growl.

"You like that place, ha?!" She let out a soft chuckle.

"Yes, they are friendly there, and the food is great." My mouth started to water as I remembered how good their food was.

"Yayas, it is then." Mom said, smiling.

"Thanks, Mom!" We all went out, and I did not say anything about what had happened in school.

My Little Shogun

Chapter 13
Kenji

LIAM

I watched the full moon from a custom window seat shaped like a half-octagon. I stared as it lit the sky and the seemingly endless fields around Grandpa's and Nana's house.

"Are you still awake, Liam?" My mom asked as she quietly entered my room.

"You can come in, Mom," I stood as she entered my room.

"Are you OK? You barely talked at dinner." She asked.

"I was just thinking of things. But I am alright." I tried to hide what was bothering me.

"You know, Liam, I never thank you for doing this. You could have chosen to stay with Soba and Grandpa Hideshi, but you thought of Grandpa and me first. For that, I am forever thankful, son. You can always count on me if you want to talk about something."

"Can I ask you a question, a serious one?"

"You can ask me anything, Mom."

"OK, I want to get to know you better. When you look at yourself in the mirror, what do you see? Describe yourself, honestly."

"Hmmm. I see a young man who has a loving mother and experienced a father's love. I see stubbornness like my mom, mixed with kindness. I don't always know what to do when confronted with challenges or problems, but I believe in myself like what my mom says to me a million times every night." I grinned.

"Oh, Liam. That's a good way to describe yourself. We believe in you, and I always will. Don't forget what you said about yourself, OK. That is what matters and not anyone else's opinion about who you are."

"Thanks, Mom."

"Goodnight, Liam."

"Goodnight," I said as my mom stepped out and quietly closed the bedroom door.

Kenji stood near where I once sat, facing the dark grass. The dark grass was how you see the green grassy fields at night lit just by the pale beams of the moonlight. He stood on top of the silhouette made by the moonbeams as they passed through the window.

"You know Liam, you probably have your reasons for not telling your mom, but eventually, you should tell her soon so that she could help you early. She would not judge you."

"I'll tell her, Kenji. I am just sorting things out. I am trying to figure out why they targeted me on my first day in school. Do I look like someone you could bully?" I stood next to him and saw my reflection on the window.

"It's not your fault that someone decided to bully you today. You did not do anything wrong to deserve that. Nobody

should bear nor endure anything like that. If you can find a way to end this early, please do so.

"Some might say that being of a different race is a reason. Others might say that you don't conform to how they look or act, so they try to bring you down to their level. In some cases, even though they are bright and look beautiful, they still get bullied out of jealousy. A few would say it's because they perceive you as weak, a loser, poor, chubby, and all the ugly labels. But the reason you get bullied is that another person decided on their own to be mean to someone. No matter what reason the bully has, it would not justify their actions. Bullies instead try to fill their inadequacies such as self-esteem by overpowering others.

"If no one cares or dares to stop bullying, it will continue. Sometimes, someone would care but is afraid to stand up against it. For it to stop, somebody, either you or someone else, needs to do something about it."

"Thanks, Kenji." I saw him still looking outside the window.

"You know, Liam, if there is such a thing as heaven, I would imagine it to be like this. It is like this dark grass."

"Heaven could be like that dark grass?" I smiled and asked as I sat back facing the glass window to see the dark grass.

"Although heaven is just right in front of you, you could not see it fully. Darkness tricks you into believing that it does not exist. You must have faith that tomorrow's sunrise will show its vastness and beauty.

"I am not sure if there is a reason for what happened to you this morning. But you, being bullied like that is never right. To overcome the hate in your heart, you must see beyond it. Be a bigger man than Bryce or me and realize that things would get better in the end. It is hard to see it now, but it will get better.

"If that boy did that during my time, he could have started a war between clans. That's one way of starting wars back then – when one person tries to overpower another and destroys whatever they had and hold dear. I was the reason for many battles that caused many deaths and suffering. I did not see that before, and I am so sorry. I thank God for giving me a chance to understand it and pay for it with my penance. If you think Bryce was bad, I was worse than him. Be better than Bryce and me, be the bigger man. Nothing good can come out of the hate you feel right now. It always ends up hurting someone else or, worse, hurting yourself. Hate feeds on conflict, and it will never stop. I hope you find a way out of that hate and find peace despite the turmoil it brought..."

"I understand, Kenji. I am trying not to let anger overcome me. I could have taken him down as I knew how to defend myself as a junior blackbelt. But I chose not to. That's the hard part. Like what my dad once said, that is **strike one**. I'll try to be calm and keep my reaction to his hate in check. I hope he does not bother me again."

"And if anyone tries to put a label on you or call you ugly names, mind them not. You alone can decide who you are. Don't let anyone do it for you. Don't lose yourself from bullying. You have so much ahead of you. Your life has just begun, and better things are coming your way. You need to see beyond it no matter how hard it may seem."

"OK, Kenji. I'll put my heart into it. Thank you!"

"You are welcome, son. I am always here for you." Kenji was still talking when he noticed I fell asleep by the window seat.

My Little Shogun

He sat beside me as I was unexpectedly able to sleep soundly. My once-troubled mind was able to find peace after my conversations with Kenji.

The smell of freshly burnt Guatemalan coffee was in the air. I can hear distant conversations from the kitchen as I brush my teeth. Toasted bread and omelets filled the breakfast nook. Grandpa, Nana, and Mom woke up early to have breakfast with me.

"Big day for both of you! Mom is flying grandpa's Cirrus Vision Jet for the first time, and you, Liam, are going alone to your new school here in the U.S. via the big yellow bus. I hope you both have a great day. We didn't want to miss this day." Nana talked to me as she handed me my omelet.

"Thank you, Nana. Do you want some of my omelet, grandpa? It has bacon in it." I turned to Grandpa Tristan as he turned his power wheelchair around the table and helped him transfer to the breakfast nook table.

"Nana iz herrre. I can't have it. Morrrning!" Grandpa smiled, and his speech was getting better.

"You guys seem to be in a good mood. I am glad you woke up on the right side of the bed today." Mom joked around with Grandpa while we ate together.

Thirty more minutes before I ride the yellow school bus for the first time. It was different from walking and riding the trains in Japan.

"What time is your flight with Desmond? Is everything ready with his proposal? Will you be comfortable flying the Cirrus Vision Jet of dad?" Nana asked mom.

My Little Shogun

"Don't worrry about her. That's nothing comparrred to the Herculezz C130zz, and Cezzna citation zhe is uzed to flying. Bezide, zhe had a great teacher, me."

"I will be alright, Mom. The appointment is at 10:00 AM. I hope Clarice says yes after all this effort. If she says no, it would be an awkward flight back home." Mom laughed as she gently placed her right palm on my shoulder.

"Ready, Liam? I'll wait with you outside."

"We arrre coming too," Grandpa and Nana headed out with us as we waited for my bus.

You could hear the distinct rumbling of a big engine as it turned the corner to our house. The automated red octagon stop sign unfolded itself as it stopped in front of us - the yellow bus with black parallel stripes towered over our heads. You could barely see what was going on inside it.

"See you later, Mom." I kissed her and waved at Nana and Grandpa, waving from the porch.

"Good morning, Ma'am!" I greeted the driver as I climbed up the steps.

"Good morning to you, too." Many students were already inside and were seated mainly in the middle of the bus. I was walking towards the back end when I began to stumble. If not for a student stopping my fall, I could have found myself in a horizontal position on the cold metal floor. Instead, I saw a foot sticking out as I looked back to what could have caused me to fall.

"Oops, sorry." Everyone started laughing. I almost lost it, and I was about to confront the teenager who stuck his foot out. I did not notice that Bryce was on my bus and laughed as he saw my face fuming with anger. The boy who broke my fall grabbed my hand and prevented me from doing so.

"He is not worth your time. You can sit over here with us." I hesitated for a second but gave in when the driver urged me to find a seat.

"Please be quiet and find your seats. We will be moving towards the school in a few seconds."

"*Strike two,*" I whispered to myself as I tried to calm myself down. Kenji shook his head and maintained a fighting stance. I stared at him and asked him to calm down without me saying a word.

"My name is Sebastian." I recognized him. Bryce took something from him yesterday.

"Thanks for breaking my fall. I am Liam."

"He is not worth it." He pointed to the direction where Bryce was seated.

"He has been transferring from different schools, and now he is here. I don't know the exact reason. Stay out of his way. He would make your life miserable. He once posted a picture of me on Snapchat with a loser sticker on my forehead. Kids are afraid of him."

"I am so sorry that he did that to you."

"I try my best to keep my head down and avoid him as much as possible. But I was not lucky yesterday as you have probably seen him take my lunch money." I looked at Bryce as he looked back at me with a menacing grin.

"Thanks for talking to me. Everybody ignores me as instructed by Bryce."

"No problem. I'll be your friend, Sebastian." I shook his hand, and we spent the last twenty-minute ride to school talking about my previous life in Japan.

A quarter before 10:00 AM, my mom reached the cul-de-sac where her chartered jet company was. It had a stunning see-through glass reception area where clients could wait before boarding their flights. She saw Desmond, who wore a white polo shirt with a black stripe in the middle who could not sit still beside Clarice.

"Are you OK, Desmond?" Clarice asked Desmond as he came back for the second time from the water dispenser.

"I am just nervous. It's my first-time riding in a smaller plane." Desmond did not say the real reason why he was anxious and worried. He had one hand holding Clarice's ring inside his pocket. He drank the water as he held the small black box that contained Clarice's ring.

"Oh, it will be OK. We have the best pilot. Kate will take care of us. I will be here, too." She held his hand as he finally sat beside her.

My mom made sure everything was perfect for the couple. She then grabbed the flight plan and checklist from her office before walking towards them.

"Hi, Desmond and Clarice! Everything is all set, and we are ready to go." As Mom shook their hands, she felt Desmond break into a cold sweat.

"Desmond feels nervous flying for the first time in a small plane. I told him not to worry because we are in safe hands." Clarice was trying to assure Desmond.

"Ohhh. Yes, yes, yes, the plane we have is one of the best. It's well maintained. I'll take care of you. I'll make sure the flight is as smooth as possible." I smiled at Desmond and winked at him when Clarice was not looking for a brief second.

"Shall we go? Mr. Xavior here will assist you in boarding."

"Thank you so much, Kate!" Clarice was all smiles as they followed Mr. Xavior.

The sight of the vision jet stunned Desmond and Clarice. The shade of its deep blue color depended on how the sunlight hit its exterior. Its massive V-tail had a turbofan nestled in the V. Nothing else was built quite like it.

"It's beautiful. Wow." Clarice couldn't contain her excitement as they entered the wide tall cabin.

"This is my dad's baby, and I am so happy he allowed us to use it. Desmond is his favorite client." My mom spoke to them as she glanced at her preflight checklist.

"Thank you so much, Kate. I'll thank Mr. Tristan personally when we come back." Desmond said this as my mom was preparing to take off at one end of the runway.

When mom was about to take off, the bell rang for recess. I saw Sebastian near a Maple tree. I was walking towards him when a group of taller boys surrounded him. I saw Bryce standing in front of Sebastian from a distance with his palm up as if asking for something. Bigger kids with Bryce prevented anyone from getting closer to Sebastian and Bryce.

"Where is your lunch money? Give it to me." Bryce said in a stern voice.

My Little Shogun

"Bryce, I don't have much, and it's just enough for me. I don't want to give it anymore." Sebastian answered back with a trembling voice.

"Oh yeah. So, you are tough now, ha." He then slapped the back part of his hand on Sebastian's chest. But, of course, no one saw what Bryce was doing since his friends made a circle around them to hide them from everyone's view.

"Sebastian, are you OK?" I tried to stand on my toes to see above their shoulders, but I could not see Sebastian.

"This does not concern you. Now scram, loser." A heavy-set teenager with his arm crossed across his chest intimidated me into leaving.

"Move away. And let me see…." He pushed me before I was able to finish my sentence.

While I almost fell flat on my face on the pavement, my mom was 55 minutes into her flight with Desmond and Clarice.

"We are 15 minutes away from the airport and will be circling some corn fields before we begin our approach." My mom talked to Desmond and Clarice over their headsets.

"It's so peaceful here, and the views are breathtaking." Clarice was all smiles as she looked through the window.

"Yes, it's beautiful. If you are lucky, you would see messages plowed by farmers for us to see - like the one on your right." My mom then turned the plane so that Clarice could get a better view.

"BE MY CO-PILOT. WILL YOU MARRY ME?" So said the plowed message on the cornfield. Desmond then dropped on one knee with the opened black box towards Clarice.

Clarice saw the sign and could not believe what she saw. She turned her head towards Desmond to tell him about what she had just seen. But, to her surprise, she saw a diamond ring in front of her.

"Clarice, will you be my co-pilot in life? Will you marry me?"

"YESSSS!!!" Desmond slipped the ring on her finger, and she gave him a tight embrace.

"Congratulations to you, Desmond and Clarice. I am so honored and happy to witness this moment. It's one in a million. We will be preparing our approach soon. Thank you for choosing me to be part of this."

"Thank you so much, Kate." Desmond and Clarice were still on each other's arms as they could not contain their excitement and happiness.

While my mom witnessed Desmond and Clarice's best time of their lives, I found my face inches from the pavement. Kenji attempted to help me by covering me with his body.

"You OK, Liam?" I did not hear this as I quickly stood up and pushed myself in.

SEBASTIAN! ARE YOU OK?! I shouted as I bulldozed my way in through Buck and Bret's shoulders like a bowling ball. Once I got through, I saw Bryce lifting Sebastian by his shirt. Everything happened so quickly that I did not know how I removed Sebastian from the clasp of Bryce. Sebastian fell to the ground as I stumbled a few feet from him. Our eyes met, and I would never forget the terrified look in his eyes.

"No. Stopppppp!!!" Everything seemed to be in slow motion as I saw Kenji racing towards me to shield me from being

kicked by Bryce's friends. However, I knew that Kenji would not be able to protect me, and I saw Sebastian was about to be kicked by Bryce.

Although Kenji was already on top of me, I could not remember what he uttered. I was bracing to feel a kick to my stomach when I heard an inner voice....

"Get up! Get up!"

I stood up, and I raced towards Bryce and Sebastian with all the strength that I had. I was saying to myself---**strike three**. I got to do something about this and defend myself and Sebastian.

I was about to kick Bryce, but I did not.... Instead, I threw myself on Sebastian and shielded him from the fury of Bryce's kicks. I held Sebastian close to me, and I would not let go. I don't know how many times Bryce kicked me. I was scared, and I did not know how much it would hurt. But all I cared about was to protect Sebastian.

"Fight! Fight! Fi..." The yelling stopped as the teacher started to rush where we were. Bryce and his friends hurriedly left us as soon as they saw the teacher coming.

"Everybody, back to your classroom!" Yelled a male teacher.

"Liam, get off Sebastian." Mrs. Crider said this as she tried separating Sebastian and me. "What are you doing with him? I am not going to repeat saying this... Get off Sebastian."

I did not realize that Bryce was gone, and I was still hugging Sebastian tightly. When I finally realized that Mrs. Crider was talking to us, I opened my eyes and let go of Sebastian.

"Are you OK, Sebastian?" I whispered to him.

"Thanks, Liam. I was petrified." Sebastian was still trembling as he answered back.

"Liam and Sebastian, follow me to the principal's office, and the rest of you go back to your classrooms."

Bryce and his friends turned their backs and pretended that nothing had happened. Buck, who was with them, looked back at us with a sad and worried face. Mrs. Crider then escorted Sebastian and me to sit in front of the principal's office as they tried calling our parents.

Desmond and Clarice felt the vibration of the wheels as they hit the tarmac. My mom saw them holding hands. She was happy for them. She felt a warm feeling on her chest as their love for each other reminded her of my dad, Hanzo. She smiled as she reminisced the unconditional love of my dad for her.

"Goodbye, Desmond and Clarice. I'll be back in five days to pick you up. Congratulations to you both." My mom hugged them both before she climbed aboard the Vision jet. My mom forgot that her phone was on airplane mode as she saw no messages or calls. She waited for her turn on the runway as she headed back home.

It was 1:15 PM when she returned to Chesterfield, Missouri. Mom grabbed her phone as she made her way back to her car.

"Hmmm. I forgot that I had my phone on airplane mode." When she switched it back on, messages and missed call notifications filled her screen.

"When you get this, Kate, call me as soon as possible. Something happened to Liam in school." My Nana called and

texted her several times. She was hoping that she would answer soon.

"Ring, ring, ring." Nana was calling her again.

Chapter 14
Farewell

LIAM

I sat with my eyes wide open in a state of disbelief and shock from what happened. Sebastian held his left arm with his right hand as he entered the principal's office, where his parents were waiting. He did not look at me. Instead, he had his shoulders slumped as he looked downwards.

"I am so proud of you, Liam." Kenji was beaming with pride as he talked and sat beside me. Our backs rested on the wall that divided the office and the small hallway near it.

I almost did not hear Kenji as I stared at that white wall. My mind went black like the lights in my head were not turned on.

"Proud of me?"

"Yes, Liam. What happened to you played differently in my mind. You could have taken him down and beat him up, but Sebastian was way more important than revenge. You have taught me that love overpowers hate. Helping someone desperate while putting yourself in harm's way in the process is the definition of a hero.

My Little Shogun

You became the bigger man, and no number of kicks or punches could break the strength of your character. You are indeed your father and mother's son."

The door of the principal office creaked as it opened to the opposite side where we were seated. Sebastian stopped momentarily in front of me as they got out.

"Thank you, Liam." I was about to talk to him when his parents whisked him away from me and headed home.

"Liam, wait here for a moment until your mom comes. She just called while she was driving from the airport." Mr. Davis redirected his attention to me as he finished talking to Sebastian's parents.

"I hope my mom would not be mad at me."

"Why would you say that?"

"She might think I started everything."

"Believe it or not, she listens to you. She believes in every word you say more than you think."

"I hope you are right, Kenji!"

"I hope Liam is OK. He seemed to be fine when the school bus got him. What possibly could have gone wrong in school?" My mom thought aloud when she heard car horns going off while driving. She did not notice every yellow or red light on her way to my school.

"Snap out of it, Gates!" She shook her head when she almost rear-ended a black sedan with its rear red lights on. She steered her car to her right, which caused her tire to hit the curve. There was a semi-truck traveling on the opposite side. She saw it at the corner of her eye, and everything seemed to slow down as

it happened. She had a split second to maneuver her SUV to avoid it. My mom found her SUV on top of a grassy open lot after she tried steering it to safety. She finally slowed down and was able to get to the parking lot of my school.

"I don't care what happened in school as long as he is not hurt. Please don't let him be hurt." She was praying as she entered my school. She weaved through the hallways to reach the second floor, where the principal's office was. Her fears all melted away as she saw me seated unharmed with my tattered white polo shirt with dirt on them.

"Thank God, you are OK. What happened? I was so worried." She brushed through my black hair with her fingers and held my collar bone as if trying to see if she would feel a bump or wound.

"I am OK, Mom. I am not hurt. I was just waiting for you to come before I talk to the principal." Mr. Davis saw my mom and asked us to come into his office.

"There was an incident during recess that involved him and Sebastian. Mrs. Crider, one of our teachers, found him on top of Sebastian while students were yelling, "Fight, fight." We are trying to determine what happened, and we have already talked to Sebastian, who was in a state of shock and could not recall anything.

"I was hoping that Liam could help us understand why he was on top of Sebastian. Liam, could you tell me what had happened?"

I was silent for a few seconds while figuring out what to say.

"I saw Sebastian surrounded by a group of bigger kids. I saw him fall to the ground, and my initial thought was to protect him. That's why I was on top of him. I was trying to protect him from being kicked and bullied. I know I should not meddle with other kids' business, but I felt he needed my help at that time."

"Do you know the kids who you thought were bullying Sebastian?"

"It happened so fast, and I am still new in this school. I don't even know the names of my classmates, let alone the names of the bullies. All I cared about at that moment was protecting Sebastian."

"Do you think you can identify them?" Mr. Davis asked.

"It would be hard for me because I am still in a state of shock. I am so sorry if I am not of much help."

"No, No...It's OK, Liam. You are right. You should get some rest first, and if you remember anything, like what I said before, you can come to me."

"Yes, sir." I knew who did it, and I should have told them who the bullies were. But I thought to give the bullies a chance to think about what they had done. So, I would allow them first to come forward. I wanted so badly to tell the principal who did it, but I opted not to.

"Rest assured, Mr. Davis. I'll talk to Liam and, if we find out any more information, we will let you know."

"Thank you, Mrs. Alberts."

We stood up, and I was about to go through the opened door when Mr. Davis touched my shoulder.

"Liam, you are a brave boy. Thank you for looking after Sebastian when he could not defend himself. I will never forget your kindness, and we will get through this. My door is always open. OK?"

I thought Mom would be mad at me but, instead, "You know what, Liam, I am craving for some Andy's ice cream. Do you want some?"

It took me a second, "Yes, Mom. I would love to have one." We drove to the nearest branch and got two Straw-Ana sundaes. We sat at a metal bench outside.

"Is this not the best ice cream in the world? When I was young, like you, your grandpa would take me out like this when I had a bad day in school. It always made me feel better.

"Sometimes…Don't tell your Grandpa Tristan, I would pretend to have a bad day just to have a taste of this ice cream. I am so happy sharing a moment like this with you."

"Thank you, Mom!" I said to her while wiping my sundae mustache. I wanted to keep to myself what happened, but I suddenly remembered what Kenji had told me. I need to tell Mom, and I think this was the perfect time to do it.

"Mom…" I said with some hesitation.

"Yes, Liam?" She took a large spoonful of the sundae, which was already half done.

"I need to tell you something."

"You can tell me anything. You are in a safe place, and I would not judge you."

"I had a rough start in school. Probably because I was new, or looked different, somebody decided to bully me on my first day in school. I did not tell you. I wanted to keep it to myself and try to figure out why I got bullied."

"You were bullied? Tell me what happened?"

"On my first day in school, a bigger kid shouldered me for no apparent reason. First, I am sorry I did not tell you right away. Second, remember when you waited for me to get to my school bus, the same kid, Bryce, tripped me. Thanks to Sebastian. who broke my fall, I could have fallen flat on my face."

My mom's eyes were focused intently on me, and she did not utter any word as she let me continue talking.

"Lastly, I knew who bullied Sebastian."

"Let me guess…Bryce!" My mom said without skipping a beat.

"I did not tell Mr. Davis because I did not want to be a snitch. I don't know if that kind of reasoning is right, but I decided to give them a chance to come forward themselves. Even though I think it's close to impossible that somebody in their group would spill the beans."

"Group? Group of bullies?"

"Bryce is their leader. I saw Sebastian surrounded, and I wanted to help him as he helped me when Bryce tripped me. I barreled my way through their circle and pushed Bryce's hand to give Sebastian a chance to escape. He was not able to run as he had fallen to the ground. I, too, laid beside him. Bryce and his gang of bullies were about to kick us both when I quickly threw myself on top of Sebastian. That's the reason why they found me on top of Sebastian. I was protecting him from Bryce. I did not want him to get hurt." My mom was teary-eyed as she waited for me to finish.

"First of all, it is not your fault that someone bullied you. If the bully's excuse is your looks, how you talk, how chubby, or how smart you are, that is not a valid excuse. Bullying someone is a choice. They don't understand or care how hurtful they can be when they try to fill their empty self-esteem. They think that trying to overpower you through verbal or physical force would quench their thirst for attention and acceptance. Instead, it just makes things worse.

"I am so sorry that you experienced this on your first two days in school. But unfortunately, bullies are pretty much a part of life, and as you said, learn how to deal with them without losing yourself. And if you have a caring mother and family like ours, a friend, or a person you can rely on, you should not be facing it alone. It takes a whole village to stop a bully."

"Yes, Mom. I won't hide anything from you from now on. I am so sorry that I did."

"It's OK, Liam. It's part of growing up. You will learn many things as you go along, and I, your family, and friends, will be there to guide you through it. You will learn nothing by keeping it a secret. You are better off telling people who are looking after your best interest so that you can learn and deal with it early on rather than wait until it's too late and difficult to deal with."

"No more secrets, Mom," I promised.

"So…What do you want to do with Bryce and his misfit friends?"

"I'll wait until the weekend is over. if no one comes forward, I will tell Mr. Davis before they do this to another kid."

"If you like, I could be there with you."

"OK, Mom." I hugged her tight, and we headed home to my grandparents, who were eagerly waiting for us to tell them what had happened.

After dinner, we all stayed out on the patio and roasted some marshmallows in the fire pit that Grandpa made. Nana and Grandpa were very worried, so they tried to talk to me more. I felt better after our conversation.

"I already emailed your teacher and told her that you would stay home and be back on Monday. Is that OK with you, Liam?"

"Yes, Mom. But I want to go back to school and check on Sebastian."

"Thatsz the spirrrit grrrandzon!" Grandpa Tristan swung his right hand in front of him as he made a fist gesture.

"Before you go back to school, we will go camping and fishing over the weekend." Nana chimed in.

"That sounds great." I removed the quilt that covered me and kissed everyone who was around the fire pit.

"I am tired and will sleep now. Is that, OK?" I said to everyone.

"You want me to come with you?" Mom was about to get up.

"No, I'll be fine. It's past my bedtime. Besides, I know you will check on me later." My mom grinned at my remark.

"Goodnight, Everyone!"

"Goodnight, Liam." Nana, Grandpa, and Mom, like a chorus, said goodnight. It was weird that I did not see Kenji since

My Little Shogun

I saw him in the principal's office. If he were not talking, he would usually just sit or stand beside me without saying a word.

"I wonder where Kenji is?" I said this to myself as I walked up the staircase to my room. I was surprised to see him standing in front of the window where we talked about the dark grass.

"Hey, Kenji, where were you today? It is unusual that I barely saw you with me today."

"Oh...I am sorry, Liam. I was just here waiting for you."

"Waiting? Why didn't you tell me sooner so that I could have come? Are you OK, Kenji?" It was the first time I saw him with tears in his eyes.

"There is no better way to say this, but it's time...My time has come to leave you, Liam. I am forever grateful to whoever made this possible that I could be with you for this long. I'm thankful that I had a chance to witness how great of a young man you became. I wished it would not end, but my purpose of being with you has been met.

"You have made your circle bigger than others, and you now care for others like they are your own blood. So few could think about the way you put others before yourself. What you did today in protecting Sebastian has surpassed what other great men did in their lifetime. Men and women have tried and are still trying to answer an age-old question - what could make you happy in this world? And most would never find the answer.

"You, on the other hand, single-handedly answered with a simple act of kindness. People have forgotten how to champion goodness and forgot how good it feels like to help others. They have forgotten that pursuing what is good fills our empty hearts.

My Little Shogun

You find happiness in helping others without expecting anything in return.

"*I am so proud of you. I will never forget you.*"

"I will never forget you too, Kenji!" I brushed my eyes with my hands as I could not contain my tears.

"*You will forget me, Liam. That is the deal. But that does not matter to me, since I know you will become a great man because you know what can truly make you happy. Goodbye, Liam.*"

He hugged me, and I could feel him embracing me for the first time. I felt contentment and happiness as he fades away from my sight. Kenji was gone, and little by little, my memories of my friend came and went like the wind.

Chapter 15
Full Circle

LIAM

My eyes were half-opened as I felt a warm, nurturing light on my face. Some of the morning sunbeams were dancing through the small gap between my heavy blue curtains. I could hear faint laughter and music downstairs. I felt I was the only one still in bed. I expected to have the worst sadness as I woke up but ironically, I felt refreshed. I felt like a million bucks. It was a rare feeling like what you felt when you made the last shot at winning a championship basketball game or the feeling you had when everything aligned to make your day great---from stoplights turning all green to a stranger paying for your coffee. This day is one of those days that I wished I could replicate.

It was a beautiful Friday morning. I was supposed to go to school, but my mom decided to let me stay home after what happened. I was at the wooden platform of the staircase when I got a glimpse of Grandpa and Nana through the opened French door. They were all outside on the patio, laughing as Mom brought out breakfast. They were all waiting for me.

"Well...Good morning, sleepyhead! Did you get some sleep last night? I was about to call you for breakfast." Mom greeted me as she held a plate of strawberry crepe and placed it in front of where I sat.

My Little Shogun

"Yes, I did," I answered with a chuckle.

"Look at who woke up on the right side of the bed this morning." Nana was relieved to see me laughing.

"I feel great! Sorry, I woke up late." I should not talk when my mouth was full.

"No worries. I emailed your teacher last night to confirm that you are not going to school today. We wanted to enjoy this day with you. I heard you talking last night. Who were you talking to? Do you still see Kenji?" My mom asked.

"Kenji? I don't remember who Kenji is?"

"Don't you remember that you had an imaginary friend? You named him Kenji?" My mom was surprised.

"I remember I had one before, but it's all blurry now, and I can no longer remember."

"Hmm, maybe you outgrew him. Forget I asked then. Let's just enjoy this day, shall we?"

"I would love that, Mom," I replied as I devoured my strawberry crepe.

We did not talk about what happened in school like last night. Instead, we decided to forget about our worries and tried to enjoy our day for a moment.

"Who's turn, is it?" My mom asked as she checked on her phone for messages between our mini-golf game.

"It's Nana's turn, then me," I shouted as I stood behind Grandpa Tristan.

I saw my mom scrolling down on her phone to sync in and retrieve her emails.

My Little Shogun

"Good morning, Mrs. Alberts!

I want to personally reach out to you and your son regarding new details from what happened yesterday with Sebastian and Liam.

A witness came forward and confessed that a particular group of older kids was bullying students. As I typed this email, we wanted to make sure that you know that we are dealing with it. We don't condone such behavior, and it goes against the very values of our school. Rest assured that we will make our best effort to educate and create a safe environment for our students. We never tolerate bullying in this school, and we will continue to strive to provide a safe environment for our kids to learn.

Please tell Liam I owe him a great deal of gratitude for standing up and protecting Sebastian. We should all learn from his courage and presence of mind. We want to set up a meeting on Monday to discuss how we could best move forward and learn from this. Again, thank you for your patience, and you should be proud of Liam for how he showed compassion and selflessness to Sebastian.

Mr. Arnold Davis

School Principal"

"Mom, it's your turn!"

"I am coming. Who is keeping score?" After reading the email, she placed it down without saying a word about it. She knew it could wait. We stayed late and ate dinner on a boat that offered sunset views while lazily cruising at Table Rock Lake.

"Thank you for this day, Mom."

"Who would have thought I would have a day like this after a horrible nightmare that most would have a hard time recovering from?" I thought to myself. *"When things seem so impossible, never lose hope because you will never know what could happen next."*

"You are welcome, Liam. You are welcome." She placed her right arm around my shoulders as we watched the sun retreat into the night as its orange glow slowly vanished from the horizon.

A local newspaper caught up with the story and printed an article about the bullying come Monday. My efforts to protect Sebastian did not go unnoticed. The newspaper hailed us as heroes. Honestly, I did not care much about what they wrote. All I cared about was going back to school. I heard that Bryce and his peers were all expelled. The school's action was swift. They were true to their word and stood by their decision that bullying was not welcome.

"Are you alright, Liam?" Sebastian was the first one to ask.

"Yes, I am not used to this attention. I should be the one asking if you are alright."

"I'm OK. You being my friend makes me feel OK." Sebastian said this with a wide grin. "Whatever you need, Liam, I'll be there for you. Thank you for what you did for me."

"Don't mention it. I did it because I did not want you to get hurt."

"That's what sets you apart. You care, unlike most of us. Thank you for caring."

My Little Shogun

"You can count on me, too. I'll be there when you need me. You have a friend for life whether you like it or not." I chuckled.

"Thanks, Liam."

Years passed. Sebastian and I became good friends. After what happened to us, no other student was ever bullied again in that school. Everyone looked up to Sebastian and me.

As the seasons changed, I began to enjoy the endless charm of Missouri. You could see its splendor from its never-ending hiking trails and caves built by mother nature. You could explore its beauty during summer up until the change of colors of autumn leaves that painted the hills of Branson. You could see it from the white blanket of snow during winter to bountiful lakes filled with trout and bass at the end of spring.

With all the changes during the seasons, one thing stayed magnificent and unwavering, St. Louis Arch, which stood as a beacon of hope to all who saw it. It stood tall near a church where my grandparents were married. Occasionally, you could hear the church bells ring as you try to catch a glimpse of the glistening St. Louis Arch amid the blue sky.

I have seen the beauty of Missouri time and time again through the numerous seasons that highlighted my stay in high school. Though seasons may change, my friendship with Sebastian remained steadfast. I was still friends with Emma and Ryo, but distance and time zones made communication harder. I tried to keep in touch with them throughout the years, but the distance proved a great adversary. The last time I saw them was when I vacationed in Kyoto before my Senior year. That was the last time I saw and talked to them before they moved out of Kyoto. They both got accepted at the University of Tokyo. Emiko decided to go with them. With no fault of anyone, I somehow lost contact with them as everyone was trying to become the best of who they could be. Sometimes I would remember and attempt to reconnect with them. But there would always be something that would come up that would prevent me from doing so.

"Ready for tomorrow, Liam?" Mom walked into my room as I prepared my clothes and toga for my graduation the next day.

"Yes, Mom."

"I could not believe it. Time flew by so fast. Ten years ago, you first stepped into this room, and tomorrow you will graduate with *summa cum laude* honors in Aerospace Engineering. I am so proud of you, Liam!" She hugged me while she sobbed on my shoulder.

"Thank you, Mom! I am who I am now because of you and Dad. Without you, I would never have made it. Thank you for being there for me. I wish dad could see me graduate." I had tears in my eyes.

"He would be watching you from heaven, and if he were here, he would never stop telling you how proud he is of the kind of man you have become. You remind me of him." I could not reply as I remembered my dad as I hugged my mom again.

"Congratulations, pumpkin!" Grandpa Tristan walked in with a cane and touched my left shoulder.

"We are so proud of you!" Nana chimed in, and all of us were in a group hug. I brushed my tears away and said thank you again. That day was second to the happiest moment in my life.

For several years I worked with Boeing here in Missouri. The pay was great, and the camaraderie in our team of engineers was unbeatable. I became one of their best lead engineers, and I

My Little Shogun

was in line for another promotion. But, despite the success I had with them, I felt that something was still missing. And I could not figure out what it was during that time.

It was almost the end of July, and I was still at work celebrating the success of streamlining a top-secret corporate project. The company treated us to a huge party, and I have been there for several hours now. I still held my first drink, which has been half-filled for a while. Everyone was having a great time, and I felt happy for them. But inside, I felt exhausted. I was thinking of ways to make an excuse to leave the party.

"It's a great party. Do you want me to get you another champagne, Sir?" A waiter noticed I had been holding my glass for a long time.

"Ring, ring, ring." My phone rang, and it was my mom.

"No, thank you!" I then answered my phone. "Hi, Mom! Mom, I am still at the party. I'll call you back in a few minutes, OK?"

"OK, Liam."

I told my fellow engineers that I was heading out. I told them I had to leave early. They were all so busy laughing and drinking that they barely noticed me leaving.

"Thanks, Mom, for calling me. I needed to get out of that party."

"Why? You should be celebrating. Congrats for a job well done."

"I know... I just feel exhausted." My mom heard the wind as I talked to her on my phone while driving with my windows opened.

"It sounds like you are driving. Get some rest, and we will talk later. Congrats again, Liam."

"Thanks, Mom. I'll talk to you later." Mom hung up, and she wanted me to concentrate on my driving. The moment I placed my phone down, "Norah Jones-Nightingale" played on the radio. It was the favorite song of my Grandpa Tristan. This song somehow reminded me of my dad.

"I love you, Dad, wherever you are. I miss you." I pulled into my garage. I was home.

I had one of those nights when my body was so exhausted, but my mind was still running without any sense of need for sleep. With my blue suit still on, I wandered into my office. My laptop lit up and sounded an alert for a recently received email. I removed my jacket and placed it at the backrest of my black chair. I sat and wondered, *"Who might be emailing me at this late hour?"*

It was a 3D pop eCard with *"The Golden Pavilion"* silhouette and a white cherry blossom near the center, with a pink background and dark grass at the bottom. The email did not say anything but had a beautiful purple butterfly. I scrolled to who had sent it.... It was from Emma.

"It has been a while since I got an email from her. My Emma probably remembered me. I should reply. But what would I say? She did not say anything or ask for something. Maybe I should send another eCard or maybe not."

I was hesitant and did not know how to respond to her. But I am certain, although it has been a long time since we talked, I sure miss her. I wondered how her life turned out to be.

My Little Shogun

I was about to email her back when I caught a glimpse of the following email. Kiyoshi, the boy who gave me the lantern during my dad's funeral to float in the river, had sent an email, too. I got curious and opened it up before I replied to Emma.

It was a letter with Mitsubishi Aircraft Corporation as the header.

"Good evening to you, Liam!

I hope this letter finds you well. You might be surprised by my sudden correspondence, but I wish to offer you a proposition. I have been following your career for years, and you could help us expand our company. I was fortunate enough to head several teams of aerospace engineers. Therefore, I would like to see if you would consider a vice president position in our company. The CEO and Board of Directors are entirely on board with this offer, and they wanted me to reach out to you, personally, since they knew that I had known you way back.

I wanted to let you know how much I value you and your family. I respect what your family represents and your dad's legacy here in Japan. I am so happy to see that you are so successful, and I would like to reconnect with you one way or the other.

If you decide to come and visit us, please let me know. All expenses will be paid whether you accept our offer or not. The mere fact that you come and consider it would be a great honor to us.

Thank you,

Kiyoshi"

After responding to Emma with a St. Louis Arch, wish you were here eCard, I responded to Kiyoshi.

My Little Shogun

"I would love to come and visit." I know it was an impulsive decision, and I was so comfortable with my life here in Missouri. But the mere thought of going back to Japan made me happy. I don't know why it sparked a fire in my idle heart. It felt like I was coming home after being away for such a long time.

The next day, I made my way to Mom's house, where I had breakfast on a Saturday morning.

"Mom, I need to tell you something."

"Tell me what, Liam?" As she gave me an omelet and pancakes again.

"Remember Kiyoshi? He emailed me last night. He wanted me to consider a vice president position in their aircraft company in Japan. I was considering it. Of course, I would first check it out, but I have strong feelings that I will accept it."

"I knew from the start that there is a big chance of you going back to Japan. It was the only place that I have seen you the happiest. Plus, you will be closer to your Dad, Grandpa Hideshi, and your Soba. Whatever choice you make, I know that you will do it based on what makes you happy. I'll support you all the way. I was thinking of coming back there myself to be close to Hanzo. I have been away too long. Everything here is all Kosher. We sold the company with stock options. And I took care of Mom and Dad's needs. I might follow you there if you decide to take their offer."

"Thanks, Mom. I'll let you know. I'll leave next week and meet up with Kiyoshi."

It was the last month of summer when I reached Japan. Not much had changed, but every single sound or scent brought back happy memories from my childhood. Soba and Papa were so pleased that I came. I knew that before coming here that I had already made my choice. I have no complaints about where I started, and I consider Boeing one of the best companies in the world. But being in Japan made me feel alive again. The feeling of emptiness has dissipated and replaced with the unending joy of anticipation. I realized that this is the place where my contentment resides. It is where I would find my definition of happiness.

I took the job offer and decided to start mid-October after I resigned from my current job. They were sad to let me go. They wished they could do more to let me stay, but they understood why I was moving. They wanted to see me happy and succeed. Mom decided to come with me, but I would go first.

Fall was upon us. It was mid-October in Kyoto, Japan, where the leaves of the cherry blossoms showed their radiant beauty. I have traveled via the Shinkansen from Osaka, where my new company was. I was supposed to start mid-October, but they decided to push it to the end of the month. They wanted me to enjoy the Jidai Matsuri festival where my dad played Gamo Ujisato. Before the festival, I decided to come early and stay with my grandparents. I made plans to visit the Golden Pavilion. It has been a while since I last saw it and I remembered how beautiful it was.

I was enjoying my Matcha green tea latte when I heard a familiar voice.

"Is that you, Liam?" I turned around and saw the most beautiful girl I had laid eyes on. I was hesitant to guess who she was at first, but once I saw her eyes, I was sure she was the girl I had been missing for a long time. Emma found me when I least expected it. She just moved back to Kyoto a month ago. She was surprised to see me while she was visiting the Golden Pavilion.

My Little Shogun

You could call it fate or destiny…. Excuse me for being mushy, but I would call it "love." I let go of her once, but never again would I allow her to go out of my sight. We talked for hours until we were the only people near the Golden Pavilion. After just a few months, I proposed to her and settled in Japan.

It has been a year since we got married, and it was New Year's Eve when we found ourselves in the hospital expecting our firstborn. Mom, Grandpa Tristan, Nana, Grandpa Hideshi, and Soba were all waiting for Emma to give birth. We were undecided yet about his name.

"I am just here for you, Emma, by your side if ever you need anything."

"I am so excited to meet our son. I am so happy to meet him finally."

At the stroke of midnight, New Year's Day, Emma gave birth to our son. The bells at the nearby Shinto shrine rang. It would ring 108 times throughout the first day of the New Year. (Joya-no-Kane). People believed that once a priest struck it for the 108th time, those who heard its' soothing sound would be cleansed of all their last year's earthly desires and vices.

Unknown to me, Kenji, who I had forgotten, was hearing the bell. He felt that he would start his journey again and be attached to my son as part of his penance.

Kenji was about to start his journey when I heard the cry of my firstborn. They let him kiss Emma first and eventually gave him to me.

"We will call him Kenji…." Barely able to speak, Emma gave the name of our son.

"Happy New Year, Kenji." I swaddled him with my arms as I rocked him back and forth. I did not realize that it was my happiest moment. Happiness has found me at last.

Kenji was ready to do his penance again, but he realized something was different this time. He felt forgiveness, and he went beyond the limits of what we knew and understood here in this world. The bell continued to ring. It rings for anyone who could hear it.

THE END